J.P. CHOQUETTE

The Pact

scared E cat

First published by Scared E Cat Books 2020

This novel is entirely a work of fiction. The names, characters and incidents portrayed in it are the work of the author's imagination. Any resemblance to actual persons, living or dead, events or localities is entirely coincidental.

First edition

*This book was professionally typeset on Reedsy.
Find out more at reedsy.com*

To YOU, dearest reader, for coming along on the adventure. I am grateful to spend time via the pages of this book, with a fellow bookworm.

Acknowledgement

Book nine and grateful thanks go out to all my readers. I'm so honored that you choose my books, tell your friends about them, and leave reviews. You really are the best!

This book wouldn't be half as enjoyable without the early readers who give such valuable feedback. My gratitude to Erin Chagnon, Michele Deppe, Pam Irish, and Angela Lavery. Thank you for giving up your free time to make this book better.

Many thanks, once again, to Helen Baggot, my excellent editor. Thank you for your valuable insights. I'm grateful also to Bespoke Book Covers which created yet another wonderful and sinister cover. Thank you for your artistic designs.

To Serge, my deep gratitude for all the long hikes in the woods and for sharing your own creative outlook—both inspire me. I'm so glad we're on this path together.

To Pascal: thank you for being patient when I'm forgetful (which is often) and for offering great suggestions when I get stuck on a book-related problem. I love your creativity and helpful ideas. And I can't wait to see your first book in print.

First and last and everywhere in between, deepest thanks to my Creator. I'm so grateful to be able to bring stories to life and share them with others.

~Dios Amore~

Chapter 1

Jude Langlois

"Well, if you hadn't dragged us up here on this stupid wilderness weekend, I guess we wouldn't be talking about this, Rick!" Mom's voice had that tight, rubber band sound to it.

"Give me a break. If we weren't fighting here, it would be at home. If it wasn't at home, it'd be out with friends. You know what your problem is?" Dad asked.

Silence. Then a snort.

Dad answered his own question. "You never let it rest."

Jude heard part of his mother's reply though the end was drowned out by his sweatshirt. Tonight, he'd use it as a pillow. Now though, he used it to block out his parents' arguing. The tent was too hot and the heavy shirt on his head made it worse. It was stuffy and the air under the sweatshirt was damp and smelled musty. But anything was better than listening to more of their argument.

When Dad had suggested the camping trip, Jude had been over-the-moon excited but acted like he wasn't. Being psyched about things, especially things you're doing with your family, definitely wasn't cool. Not when Jude was about to start fifth grade. And definitely not around his new friends.

He heard the muffled sound of his parents but now it was like listening to them underwater. Which reminded Jude, he was thirsty. If only he'd remembered to bring his water bottle into the tent with him. And his tablet, not that there was much battery left.

"No technology," his mother had warned him that morning with that raised eyebrow look that always made him feel like his clothes were suddenly too tight and too itchy. "Either of you," she'd said, swinging her gaze from Jude to Dad and back again.

"Good idea," his father had responded, whistling cheerfully as he'd rinsed his bowl in the sink. "Right, Jude?" Dad had kissed his mother's cheek when she walked past and she'd playfully swatted him.

"But what about in the car?" Jude had asked. "It's a long ride, isn't it?"

His mother, busy doing something with packages of food on the counter, hadn't looked at him. "Sure, baby. In the car on the way there. It'll eat up your battery anyway, it's a long ride."

"How long?"

"Long. Maybe two and a half or three hours."

Jude had nodded and spooned more cereal into his mouth. He'd been texting Peyton on his tablet and checked the battery. Fifty-six percent. He'd better plug it in.

Peyton: Theres a huge bat up their.

2

Jude: Where?

Peyton: Grotin. Thats where ur going rite?

Jude: Yeah

Peyton: Lookout fir it

Jude thought a moment. Then replied.

Jude: Not scared of bats

Peyton: You will be. This one eats people!!!

Jude snorted and wiped a drop of milk off the tablet.

"Whatever," he'd said, but didn't write back.

"What, honey?" His mother glanced up from the counter and the food spread out on it.

"Nothing."

"You'd better get your breakfast stuff cleaned up. We're leaving in," Mom glanced at the clock on the microwave. "Twenty minutes. And you still have to brush and bring your stuff down. I left your sleeping bag in the hall; did you see it?"

"Yeah." Jude had hurried to plug in his tablet, but it was still only at seventy-three percent when they'd pulled out of the cul-de-sac and headed for the winding backroads that led to the Northeast Kingdom.

"Isn't it beautiful," Mom had said when they'd stopped at a pull-off with a little sign that read, "Scenic View". Jude was trying to kill the last zombie when his mother nudged his shoulder.

"Jude. Look around you. You're missing it."

"Let's get a picture," Dad had said. Jude had let out a groan as the zombie killed him. He'd spent the whole trip making it to this level and now he was going to have to start all over again. He trudged out of the truck and let himself be squished between his parents.

"Smile!" his mother called.

Click. Click. Click.

It had taken a long time to get to the place they were camping. Jude noticed bright-yellow signs on the roadside warning of moose the deeper they got in the forest. His stomach had started to feel weird and his head ached a little by the time they got to the campground.

Setting up camp had been fun though. And by the time dinner rolled around (baked beans and hot dogs cooked over the fire with s'mores for dessert), Jude had forgotten all about his tablet. Him and Dad had walked down to the little creek and found crawdads and minnows. Then they'd followed the creek down further, listening to the sound of rushing water.

"What is that?" Jude had asked.

"It empties out into the lake somewhere," Dad called over the sound of the water. "We must be getting close."

And they were. They walked for about five more minutes and then the woods ended unexpectedly. Before them was the gleaming, smooth surface of the lake. The stream flowed in a rushing tumble at the edge of the lake. It fell over the downed trees and old, rotting branches there. Jude could barely see the other side of the lake where an orange sun was sinking like a big egg yolk behind the mountains.

"Beautiful, isn't it?" Mom called. She stood on the pebbly shore, looking at them with her arms wrapped around her waist.

"You beat us," Dad said, and Jude jogged toward her.

"How'd you get here so fast?"

"Magic," she said and laughed. "Also called following a path." She jerked her thumb toward a sliver of dirt tucked into the trees to her right. "Pretty, huh?" She faced the lake again and the orangey light made her face and hands and legs poking out of her shorts glow.

"I guess," Jude said.

"You guess?" She laughed and messed up his hair. He leaned in toward her, glad that she seemed happier now than earlier today. His parents hadn't fought once since they left home which was a record. Unless you counted the little spat at the gas station when Dad got a chocolate bar and soda for Jude.

"I packed healthy snacks so we wouldn't have to get anything," Mom had said. But Dad had just shrugged and handed the treats over the backseat.

Jude liked this: both of his parents now standing side by side, his dad with his arm draped over his mother's shoulders and Mom with her arm around Jude's shoulders. They stood like that for a few long seconds, watching the sun and the way it made the waves sparkle. Suddenly, Jude felt something big flew by his head. He yelped and jerked back.

"What was that?" He looked around but saw only a few birds fluttering in and out of the trees.

"Just a bat," Dad said, dropping his arm from Mom's shoulders and pointing at the dark shapes above them. "They must have a feast out here with all these bugs." Jude followed Dad's pointing finger over his shoulder. The woods were gloomy and birds flew all over the place. Not birds, he corrected himself as two more swept out of the forest. Bats.

"I learned about these in school," Jude said, trying to keep his voice normal over the hammering of his heart. "They're harmless. They eat bugs, especially mosquitoes and gnats." Thinking about that made his heartbeat slow down. They weren't like vampires and didn't want to eat him. "They've been delining in recent years. They have some sickness."

"You mean declining?" Dad asked.

Jude shrugged.

"That's true. Their numbers have been declining. There's some white-nose disease. What is it, hon, a virus they've got?"

Jude's mother shook her head.

"Anyway, biologists are trying to figure it out. To help them before they all died away."

"Peyton says there's a giant bat that lives up here in the woods. That it eats people," Jude blurted out and then wished he hadn't.

Mom and Dad exchanged a glance, both chuckling.

"Oh really?" Mom asked.

Dad draped his hands loosely over Jude's shoulders.

"Like this?" He squeezed and brought his face close to the back of Jude's neck and shoulders, making a loud *nom, nom* sound, and smacking his lips. Jude shrugged him off but was laughing.

"We'd better go," Mom said. "I didn't bring a flashlight, did you guys?"

Dad shook his head. "Yeah, let's head back to camp. Before the Godzilla bat finds us," he laughed and bumped Jude's shoulder with his own.

Jude rolled his eyes but stayed where he was, watching the bats for a few more seconds. They swooped down out of the tall pine trees and flew frantically over the lake, dipping down to catch bugs he assumed, before flapping hurriedly back up. They were kinda cool. And he felt sort of bad for them because everybody hated them. Maybe when he got back to school, he'd tell Ms. Pelsky he wanted to do his report on bats.

"Jude, come on," Mom called and Jude ran to catch up with his parents' retreating figures.

Chapter 2

Marion Langlois

H ad Rick always been like this? Marion turned over on her side, the sleeping bag underneath her whispering in the moonlit tent. She'd been listening to him snore for at least twenty minutes and imagined reaching over and pinching his nose shut, keeping her palm firmly over his mouth.

It had started out as a good trip—they'd only had a couple of little spats and the evening around the campfire and then down at the lake had been good. She'd felt more relaxed—and Rick had been too—but then he'd made that comment back at the camp while she was cleaning up. Money. It always came back to money. How hard he worked to get it and how easily she spent it.

"Are you sure you know what you're getting into?" Mother had asked her the morning of her wedding. Marion still remembered the hot anger that had stuck in her throat like coffee swallowed too fast. Her mother was a snob though, and Marion had brushed off her concerns. She'd told herself it was just sour grapes. David, after all, was the man Mother and Daddy had wanted their only daughter to marry. But Dull

"You're not going to fail if you take a few weeks off here and there."

"It's not just the time away. I need to keep myself focused, keep my head in the game."

"You act like this is…I don't know. The stock market or something. It's just a—" her voice faltered.

"Just a what?"

"Nothing."

"What? Go ahead and say it. Grease monkey shop?"

"That's not what I was going to say."

"No? But, it's what you think, right?"

He'd turned away, angrily stuffing a box of graham crackers into the box so hard the edge of the box got smashed.

"…like your mother," he muttered.

"What?" Heat had flared in Marion's chest and she'd stalked over to Rick, turning him toward her. "What did you say?"

"Nothing."

"I heard you. And I'm not like my mother. Take it back!"

He hadn't responded. Just muttered, "I'll take care of this," and hauled the bear box containing every scrap of food they'd brought to the far side of the campsite. It was a remote campground, only accessible by hiking in or via the lake. They'd hauled all of their stuff in a canoe. Marion had watched him and talked herself out of flying at him or stalking off into the dark, though both had been tempting.

And now they'd be together for three more days and two nights. Stranded in the middle of nowhere.

Where's your sense of adventure now, Marion? a little voice asked her. She ignored it and tried to find a more comfortable spot on the rocky ground.

***

Marion wasn't sure how long she'd slept but she had to pee. Badly. She struggled half in and half out of consciousness, trying to talk herself into falling back asleep. It was no use though. Her bladder was not going to be put off. Propping herself upright, she struggled to find a flashlight in the dark.

Hurry, hurry, hurry. She hadn't wet the bed since she was six and didn't want to now.

Where was the stupid flashlight?

Forget it.

Sighing angrily, she crept over the sleeping form of Jude and unzipped the tent. The sound was deafening in the quiet night. Marion held her breath, worried the sound would wake Jude. No one in the tent stirred though. Even Rick had stopped snoring.

The air outside the tent was cool and smelled delicious: like being dropped into a Christmas tree. Marion fumbled around the little mat by the tent's door and stuffed her feet into canvas deck shoes, then hurried off into the woods. Jude typically slept lightly and she didn't want him shining his super-strength flashlight out here and catching her in the act.

She relieved herself behind a tree and afterward, while zipping up her shorts, looked up. The moon was three-quarters full and cast everything in a bluish wash. God, it was beautiful here. Crickets and the *glug-glug-glug* call of some far-off frogs the only noise. How long had it been since she'd been out this late at night? Her twenties, maybe. But then she'd been stumbling to a cab from a party, so full of alcohol and smoke that she wouldn't have appreciated the cool, tranquil night air.

Another noise filled the air. Soft at first, then getting louder as though something was coming toward her. Overhead the wind whispered through the trees. Maybe that had been all she'd heard. The trees, their branches moving against each other. Marion took a step, then another, and stopped.

That's what was wrong, she realized. Although she could hear the wind in the trees there was no breeze on her skin. The air was still and cold. Taking a few more steps back, Marion looked up overhead again. She gasped. Hundreds of bats filled the air. They swept down and up and strange, zigzagging patterns. Nearly colliding with each other, they raced against the indigo sky and careened in all directions. Marion darted instinctively through the trees, trying to provide some cover between herself and the bats.

Her heart cartwheeled in her chest. She hadn't said anything earlier, not wanting to scare Jude, but she'd always hated bats. Their strange, erratic movements and their tiny, jagged teeth. Their translucent wings, papery yet fibrous at the same time. People had told her that the brown bats here in Vermont were gentle, timid creatures. But she didn't believe it.

Anyway, what kind of insect population would draw so many bats to one area, Marion wondered, shoving branches out of her way before they scraped at her face. Did mosquitoes or gnats or any other bugs besides butterflies migrate? Maybe moths did. Maybe they were feasting on those and Marion just couldn't see them. She took a few more steps in the trees, feeling safer with a canopy between her and the flying mice. Peeking out from beneath the branches a few minutes later, Marion saw that the sky was still thick with them. It seemed like more had appeared in just a few minutes since she'd first noticed them.

12

Well, she couldn't stay out here all night, hiding in the trees. She flipped up the collar of her shirt, tucking her hair down the back of it. She'd heard horror stories of bats flying into long hair and then biting and clawing the person as it struggled to free itself. Marion shivered and walked more quickly back to camp, keeping one eye on the swarm of bats overhead.

Several minutes later, Marion stopped. She turned around, squinting into the darkness. Where was the tent? Heartbeat quickening, Marion pivoted and did a full, slow circle. All around her were trees. But where was the one that was closest to their site? She'd never camped at a place this remote before. Rick thought that Jude would love it—a real boys' adventure—but honestly, Marion would have jumped at the chance of a country bed & breakfast with a nice pool for Jude.

There! That tall, twisted tree looked familiar. Marion remembered its bent trunk from when they'd first gotten to the site. She walked toward it, confident that their tent was just on the other side, tucked into a tiny clearing between the other towering trees. But Marion was wrong. When she got there, she saw only more trees and more tall grasses and low-lying shrubs. She turned again. Now her heart pounded hard.

Calm down. Just calm down. She told herself this over and over, but her hands had started to shake as she wiped them on her shorts. How could this have happened? She hadn't gone that far from the tent. She had to be close now, closer than she thought. Maybe she should call out. Try to wake Jude or Rick. Just a few more minutes. The thought of Rick's face when she explained that she'd gotten lost going to the bathroom was enough to straighten her spine and dispel some of the fear.

Maybe she'd already walked past it. Could she have skirted

13

the little clearing somehow? There were other tent sites in the campground…the problem was Marion had no idea how to find them. As a remote site, there were no bathrooms, no showers, and the distance between each campsite was large to ensure both privacy and a real "backwoods" type experience. But there had to be other campers here somewhere. She just had to find them. And if she came to a site, she could follow it to the main path.

Marion took a few steps to the right, hesitated, then went left. She heard the sound of water faintly and thought it was coming from the left-hand direction. When they'd been at the lake earlier tonight she remembered the brook emptying into the larger body of water. That's where she'd go. Once she was at the lake she'd get her bearings and easily be able to find the path to follow back up to their campsite.

Feeling foolish more than afraid, Marion walked faster. Sure enough, the sound of the water gurgling and rushing grew louder the closer she got. Branches scraped her arms and twigs snatched at her bare legs, but she ignored these and continued plowing through the undergrowth.

Finally, pushing through some extra-thick pine branches, Marion found her feet sinking into the pebbly stones that made up the beach area. She laughed in relief and walked out a few more feet. It felt good to be out of the woods. To feel the air around her instead of the thick tangle of branches and pine needles and leaves rasping against her skin. Clouds had covered the moon partially, and it was harder to see now. Glancing up instinctively, Marion gasped.

It wasn't clouds that obscured the moon, she realized in disbelief. It was bats. Clouds and clouds of them. Thick and black and menacing, they swooped and pivoted, rose and dove down again. A sound came from overhead. Dread crept along Marion's backbone. She was half-tempted to turn and run back into the woods. But like a car wreck, her eyes were drawn to the sky.

Giant wings flapped. A sound like the blade of a helicopter filled the air. Marion tried to process what she was seeing. A mammoth bat.

No. No, that was impossible.

Her brain screamed at her to *get down, get down.* Marion dove for the ground and covered her head instinctively with her hands. The bat swooped down from the big pine tree she'd been standing under. She wondered dumbly how long it had been perched there if it had been watching her the whole time.

For several silent seconds, Marion thought she'd outwitted it. There was nothing. No sound. No feeling of anything looming over her prone figure. But then fire-like arcs of pain tore across her upper back and shoulders. It was unlike anything she'd ever known before. Like a volcano spewing lava. It hurt so much that the scream ended halfway out of Marion's mouth.

With its huge talons, the bat lifted her, up, up into the air. Marion hung suspended, tried to breathe. She opened her mouth again to scream but only a half-sobbing gasp came from her lips. The bat's wings thrummed in the dark sky and rose above the treetops. And Marion's world turned black.

Chapter 3

Rick Langlois

"I'm sure Mom's fine, buddy," Rick said and handed Jude a plate filled with a toaster pastry, unheated. He'd wanted to make a big breakfast: eggs, toast, bacon, but Jude insisted that they look for Marion. "Eat up and we'll head down to the lake, get a little fishing in." Rick kept his tone light purposefully.

Jude stared at the plate as though it contained maggots. "I'm not hungry. I want to go look for Mom," he said again.

Rick sighed. How do you explain to a ten-year-old that sometimes adults do dumb things? Like, walk off in a huff because they're mad at their spouse. This wasn't the first time Marion had done something like this. Once, when she and Rick had gone on a long-weekend trip to New York City, they'd fought. Rick couldn't even remember what it was about. But Marion had left the hotel in a tizzy. She'd returned hours later—and about six hundred dollars poorer—and they hadn't said much more about it. Back then the makeup sex used to be great. Now it was nonexistent.

"At least drink your cocoa," Rick said. "You need something in your belly."

Dutifully, Jude sipped from the enamel cup but his eyes over the rim were worried.

He put the cup down on the table. "Mom wouldn't just leave. Something must have happened to her."

"How about this," Rick said. "We'll finish breakfast and head down to the lake. I have a feeling your mother is down there, watching the sunrise or sketching or something like that."

"The sun rose like hours ago, Dad."

Rick shrugged. "But I'll bet you she's down there. And once we find her, we'll pack up and go for a hike, okay?"

Jude shrugged but nodded.

They cleaned up in record time—Rick wasn't really hungry either—and followed the narrow trail through the woods and down to the lake. The campsites at Osmore Pond Recreation Area were remote, meaning you didn't drive to them and you didn't have access to things like public toilets or showers. On the plus side, you also didn't have to listen to your neighbor's radio or worry about getting run over. Rick had been rough camping since he was a kid. Marion would have preferred staying at a regular state campground, or even better, at the nearest Hilton.

"Look, Dad," Jude's voice was excited and snapped Rick back to the present. His son was bent over the beach, peering at the stones and coarse sand underfoot.

"Whatcha got?" He sidled up next to Jude.

"Footprints," Jude pointed.

Rick followed his son's finger. He was right there were some full-size and some partial footprints near a big, old pine tree.

"That doesn't mean anything, son. Anyone could have come down here and left those."

"I thought you said this was our own private beachfront?

17

That the other campsites were too far away to bother us here?"

"Well, it would be inconvenient, sure. But other campers could come down here if they wanted."

Jude followed the prints further and Rick followed his son.

"It looks like there was a struggle," Jude went on, not listening to Rick. "See how the prints sort of twist and walk all over themselves?" Jude had been obsessed with these detective books that had been turned into a TV series lately. Rick was about to tell him he'd be a good P.I. himself one day when his son cried out.

"Look, Dad." He rushed to a spot a few feet down the beach. He squatted and pulled something out of the sand. Holding it up triumphantly, Jude said, "Do you believe me now?"

It was a shoe, a beige canvas shoe with tiny, navy blue anchors all over it.

Marion's shoe.

But no Marion.

Rick rubbed a hand over the back of his neck.

Dammit.

"Okay," he said in a level voice. "So, maybe Mom went swimming."

They both turned toward the water. It was perfectly calm and smooth, the reflection of the trees creating a mirror image on the surface. But no one was out on the lake, at least not in the near vicinity.

"The bat got her," Jude said, so quietly that Rick almost missed it. "Peyton was right."

"There is no giant bat, Jude."

"Peyton says there is. He read about it in a library book. It must have gotten Mom. That's why we can't find her. That's what she was struggling with." He pointed back to the mussed sand.

"Woah, hold on, buddy. Let's not jump to conclusions."

"Well, what do you think happened then?" Jude crossed his arms, his brows pulled together. He looked so much like Marion with that expression, Rick had to look away.

"I don't know. But I don't think it involves a giant, man-eating bat. Maybe she went for a walk and got turned around. People get lost in the woods all the time. Or maybe she was down here sketching and saw something—some cool animal—and went off after it, trying to get a picture so she could draw it later. You know she likes drawing that way most of the time, from pictures—"

"So, why'd she leave her shoe?" Jude wagged it at his father.

Rick swallowed. Why would Marion leave behind a shoe? A sick feeling had sprouted in his gut and now began to spread through his abdomen. What if she was in trouble? Not by a huge bat, but by another hiker? What if there was some crazy mountain man out here who'd grabbed Marion off into the woods? Was holding her against her will?

But no, that was stupid. He was being stupid. She'd left in a huff, probably irritated with his snoring—as if he could help it—and gone off to be alone and sulk. Who said she'd even been wearing those shoes? Knowing Marion, she'd probably packed six pairs. Maybe this was here from when they'd visited the lake last night. Or maybe she'd stuck a spare pair in her bag and one had fallen out. Still, Jude was upset. And Rick knew their son wouldn't be able to relax until he was sure Marion was safe. He was a worrier, that boy, something Rick hoped he'd grow out of.

"All right, here's what we're going to do," Rick said. "We're going to head back to camp and grab our packs. And then we're going to look for your mother. If we haven't found any other signs in an hour or so, we'll head back to the part of the park where I can get a cell phone signal. And then I'll call the authorities. But buddy?" Rick put a hand on his son's thin shoulder and squeezed it. "Don't worry. I'm sure that she's fine."

Jude nodded and averted his gaze when tears started to fill his eyes.

Anger washed over Rick, hot and hard. Bad enough that Marion had gone off to prove a point to him. Did she have to hurt their son in the process?

***

They looked for two and a half hours. Jude was complaining about blisters and bugs by the time they stopped. They'd been making widening circles away from their camp.

"Keep your eyes peeled," Rick had said more than once when Jude started flagging. Poor kid wasn't used to so much physical activity. His adventures consisted of running from zombies in video games. If he could have used his fingers to get him around, he'd be all set. Rick himself was struggling. He'd put on twenty pounds in the past couple of years, his daily gym time being slowly replaced with business tasks and he knew his face was red and sweaty. He could feel drips of sweat running down his back and tried to keep his voice light and reassuring. Inside though, he cursed his wife and her selfishness.

He shouldn't be surprised though. He'd loved Marion deeply when they'd married but he'd known even then that struggling with her rich-girl attitude would be a lifelong challenge. He'd never doubted that she loved him, then at least. But he'd also never forgotten what his brother had told him the night before his wedding.

"You know she's marrying you in part to get back at her parents, don't you?"

Rick had laughed it off, slugging his brother on the shoulder and ordering another round for them. He hadn't believed it then. Or at least, had been able to ignore the little tickle of truth that had wedged itself into his brain.

Marion had been everything he'd been looking for: sweet, charming, creative, and determined to make a beautiful home for them. She'd worked as the curator of an art gallery the first eight years they'd been together. But she'd given up the job to raise Jude. And while Marion's parents had never gone out of their way to make Rick feel included in the family, things had gotten better after Jude had come along. He thought about his parents who'd died in quick succession—one to diabetes, the other heart disease—when he was in his early twenties. He'd wondered often when Jude was small what they would have thought of him, what kind of grandparents they would have been. He saw his two sisters and older brother infrequently, having little in common with any of them. Besides, work was just too busy.

That was something Marion didn't understand: how many hours it took to make Langlois Auto Body successful. She thought you could just make a few decisions, toss some money at a manager, and be done with it. In reality, the business was like another child—a demanding one—that needed a lot of time, attention, and feeding. But it would be worth it. Someday Rick hoped to pass the business on to Jude.

"...can we?" his son's voice interrupted Rick's thoughts.

"What?"

"I need a drink. And a snack. Can we stop for a little while?"

Rick glanced around. If there had been another clue of Marion's whereabouts, he probably missed it. Where the heck were they anyway? He glanced distractedly at the map and his compass. GPS units didn't work this far out.

"Dad?"

"Yeah, sure." Rick glanced up from the map. "We can rest for a while. Do you see a good spot?"

"Over there," Jude pointed to a fallen log. "I want to take my pack off. It's hurting my shoulders."

Rick nodded. "Lead the way."

They settled on the big log, ferns swayed nearby. It smelled of the smell of damp, rotting wood. Marion would be warning them about the dangers of ticks, but Rick was as relieved as Jude to sink onto the log and rest his legs. While Jude sipped water and munched on a granola bar, Rick looked more carefully at the map.

"Are we going to go call for help soon?" Jude asked.

Rick sighed. "Maybe."

"We should, Dad. You said we'd look for only an hour and it's way past that."

Rick didn't say anything, just nodded and took a long swig from his water bottle.

They were quiet a few minutes, the only sound that of birds chattering in the trees and the crinkle of Jude's wrapper.

Feeling more confident about their location—they were just west of Owl's Head Peak—Rick bit into an apple and chased the bite down with another long swallow of water.

"Hey, look, Dad," Jude said excitedly, pointing toward the mountain that rose above them. "Doesn't it look like the

Lonely Mountain?"

Rick chuckled. "Sure." They'd started reading the Tolkien book together—was it *The Hobbit* or *Lord of the Rings*?—but then Rick suggested they watch the movies. The books were longer than he remembered as a kid and most nights after work he was too tired to read, the words squiggled on the page as his eyelids got heavy.

"I want to get a picture," Jude said. "Can I use your phone?"

Rick retrieved it from his back pocket and handed it to Jude.

"Hang on, I have to get a little closer to get away from these branches," Jude mumbled and walked a few long paces to the right.

"There, that's better." He snapped a couple of pictures, fiddling with the zoom function while Rick finished his apple and tossed the core far into the trees.

"Dad?" Jude asked.

"Yeah, buddy," Rick said and stood, stretching his back. Every muscle in it felt tight.

"You've gotta see this." Jude's voice was quiet and Rick felt that same sick feeling in his belly that he'd felt down at the beach. He walked to where Jude was standing and took the phone from him. The picture was so enlarged that it wobbled slightly.

"Over there," Jude said and pointed in the frame toward the mountain to their right.

Rick saw a pile of stones, a few big boulders, and lots and lots of trees.

"What am I looking at?"

"That," Jude said. He was close enough that Rick could smell his breath, a mixture of oats and chocolate. "See that opening? Look right there," he pointed to the far right of it.

Rick squinted. He needed his reading glasses to see what Jude was pointing at—then he saw it. A scraggly bush, maybe a thorn bush, perched near a jagged hole in the side of the mountain. Or maybe it was a cave's entrance.

Hanging from a branch on the bush was something red. Rick squinted again. It was a piece of red plaid. Just like the shirt Marion had been wearing last night.

Chapter 4

Jude Langlois

Something was wrong. Why would Mom be hiking way up here? And why would a piece of her shirt be outside this creepy, dark cave? Jude swallowed and tasted something bitter. He suddenly wished he was back home. That it was just a regular Saturday morning and he was playing a video game while Dad mowed the lawn and Mom caught up on laundry or wrote out the grocery list. He wished they'd never come on this trip.

"Let's check it out," his father said.

Jude nodded and started walking toward the cave.

There were rocks everywhere, and they had to pick their way through them which made them go really slow. Still, Jude kept looking around for any bare patches. Maybe he'd see more of his mom's footprints.

"Wait a second," Dad said quietly when they got to the cave's opening. Jude stopped. His father looked worried. Lines creased his forehead and his skin looked whiter than usual. Still, he smiled at Jude. Trying not to scare him, Jude guessed. Was Dad scared? Because if he was, Jude was going to be really, really scared. Dad wasn't scared, like, ever.

"We should make a plan. Chances are your mother is just up there exploring," Dad nodded to the cave above them. "But there could be animals around that might not want us in there."

But if there are animals that don't want us around, Jude thought, why would Mom be in the cave? He didn't say anything though, just nodded.

"Let's go nice and slow and keep an eye out for anything that could cause trouble, all right?"

Jude nodded again.

"I'll go first. You stay close to me." Dad tightened the straps on his pack and smiled at Jude. "Don't worry, buddy. Everything's going to be fine."

Jude followed his father to the cave. It took longer than he thought it would and they were both breathing hard when they stopped outside the cave. Jude ran ahead of his father the final few yards and reached on tiptoes to get the little piece of red fabric that fluttered in the breeze. It was too high up though. Jude felt tears form in his eyes and blinked hard, then turned away when his dad caught up to them.

His father didn't say anything, just reached up slowly and tugged at the flannel until it came free. Then he handed it to Jude. He clapped his other hand, big and warm, onto Jude's shoulder.

Jude sniffed and rubbed his arm over his eyes.

"Don't worry," Dad said again, but Jude heard fear in his father's voice. "Come on," he said and pulled Jude toward the cave's opening.

It looked small on the outside, but once they ducked into the entrance, it got really wide. It smelled weird too like it did after a really rainy night.

"Wow," Jude whispered. He was glad the dimness inside hid

the wetness on his face. He rubbed his sleeve over his face again and looked around.

"Yeah," Dad said over his shoulder. "Pretty amazing."

The cave looked like a big auditorium inside. The ceiling of it rose high up over their heads and even though it was dark, it also felt dry. Jude had been in other caves before, but they'd always felt damp and cool. This one was dry, the floor lined with sand and pebbles, just like the beach.

If he'd been in a joking mood, Dad probably would have started humming the *Batman* theme song. But Jude figured Dad was as worried as he was.

"Watch your step," Dad said a second before Jude tripped on a log. He caught himself before falling on his face. "Let's get our flashlights."

It took a few seconds for them to find the lights in their packs. Jude noticed that Dad also pulled out his big bowie knife and strapped on the leather holster he wore around his leg. It reminded Jude of when they used to go hunting. They hadn't gone for so long. Dad had been too busy—either working at the shop or catching up on work around the house—to go hunting or fishing or anything else lately.

Jude felt safer, seeing the knife. Still, everything in the cave was scary. It felt like going down into the basement when he was younger. There were strange sounds—rocks clinking when they stepped on them, but other noises too, ones Jude couldn't place. And around every rock, he expected to see a set of glowing eyes or hear a growl or feel hot breath on his neck.

"Let's keep going," Dad said, and Jude fell into line behind him again.

They walked in silence, other than the occasional, "careful," from Dad, or "watch your step here." The cave narrowed, going from the gigantic room into more of a tunnel. It was still high though. Way up overhead, Jude could see dark stones if he tipped his head up that way. He wondered if this was how miners felt when they went into caves to work every day. Did they feel this same sick feeling in their bellies, or did they get used to it?

"It gets narrow in through here," his father said, barely whispering. "Stay close."

As if Dad needed to tell him that. Jude was so close he was practically getting a piggyback ride. The tunnel narrowed a little more then broke off in two directions. How far did it go back anyway?

"Which one, buddy?" Dad asked.

Jude looked at the tunnels. They all looked the same to him. He had no idea which one Mom would pick.

"The one on the right," he said. He wasn't sure why, but it felt like that was the one Mom would have chosen.

"All right."

They picked their way over the larger stones that now littered the floor. It made it much harder to walk and Jude had to climb over some of them, they were so big. The tunnel got even smaller and Jude thought he'd picked the wrong one. They would have to turn back soon. The walls of rock were becoming tighter and tighter.

Finally, Dad stopped. "I think we'll have to try a different one."

Jude nodded and started to turn around.

"Hang on," Dad said, his voice a loud whisper. "What's that?" He pointed to something ahead on the right. There was a small opening. And there, stuck between two stones was a little, red piece of fabric.

"Mom's shirt," Jude breathed. His heart started to pound even harder in his chest. "She left it for us. It's a clue!"

"Shh," Dad said and Jude swallowed hard.

"Let's see if we can't get through that opening. We'll leave the packs here."

Jude didn't want to take his pack off and he definitely didn't want to crawl through the narrow opening that was ahead of them. He'd seen some spiderwebs and a few bugs with lots of legs and shiny backs scuttling away from them in the dark tunnel. The thought of getting on his belly and crawling through the tight space ahead of them made his stomach churn like when he rode the Ferris wheel at the fair every August. But what if Mom was on the other side? She might need their help.

"Okay," he said. "I can go first."

"No, I will," Dad said. "But you stay close behind me, all right?"

The tunnel had funneled upward so that even though the space was narrow it was high up off the ground. They had to go around rocks of all sizes, some boulders, others sharp and jagged slabs, to get to the opening in the stone. The little piece of Mom's shirt was up there, toward the top. Jude tried not to imagine her being carried in the jaws of some wolf or mountain lion. He tried not to picture her crying and scared, in this weird, gross tunnel all alone. Any fascination he'd felt in the big open area when they'd started was long gone.

A stone loosened by his dad's boot tumbled down behind him and narrowly missed Jude's hand.

"Sorry," Dad whispered loudly over his shoulder. "You all right?"

"Yeah."

Dad looked funny. He squirmed and twisted himself, trying to get his big arms and chest and belly through the narrow opening.

"I'm almost through—"

Jude saw his father's legs and big boots one second. The next they were gone.

"Dad?" he whispered loudly. "Dad?" he called out in a loud voice.

There was no answer.

Jude crawled forward. He managed to launch himself into the hole. The rocks and stones scraped his arms and legs and part of his back. His tongue stuck to the roof of his mouth and he panted slightly like he did after they ran laps in gym.

"Dad? Are you okay?"

"Watch out!" Dad's voice called out seconds before Jude tumbled headfirst into a huge, black cavern.

Chapter 5

Marion Langlois

Marion tried to roll over in bed, but something was digging into her side. She frowned as a strange smell filled her nose. It was sharp, like ammonia mixed with something sickly sweet. She'd smelled this scent before. But where? And why did her arms and legs feel so strange?

Turning over on her side, Marion opened her eyes. All around her was darkness. As her eyes adjusted she made out dark, lumpy shapes. Rocks. Boulders and stones really, some jagged and some smooth. She turned her neck further. Pain ran down her back in a sharp arc of blue lightning. She moaned, catching a glimpse of the large, flat boulder she was laying on. Around it was littered dozens of smaller ones. Marion tried again to turn over but her arms and legs didn't cooperate. Why was that?

Slowly, carefully so that she wouldn't feel the same pain again, she turned her head to look at her arms. They were coated in a thick, black ooze. She sniffed close to one of them and gagged. That's where the smell was coming from.

Where was she?

Her head felt fuzzy and thick like it was stuffed with a big pillow. She shook it and the same pain radiated down her neck and shoulders. When she moved her head it burned, hot and twisting, like someone was jabbing heated metal into her skin.

Turning in increments kept the worst of the pain at bay. The thick ooze was warm and pressed down on her arms but Marion wriggled free ignoring the fiery screams of her arms and head.

"Help!" she called out. The sound of her voice echoed around the stones and bounced away. Finally, her right arm slipped free of the disgusting, smelly goo. She lifted her arm toward herself, wincing at the pain in her shoulders. It felt as though they'd been cut open. Warmth trickled from them as she moved.

Marion suddenly felt like she was going to vomit. She stopped moving, waited for her stomach to calm. Seconds later, she gingerly explored her shoulders with the fingers of her free hand. Her shirt was tattered and both shoulder blades were crusted with blood that was matted to the cloth. She gasped, feeling large, long cuts above the bones in her shoulders and down her back.

What in the hell had happened to her? She closed her eyes. *Think. Think. Think.*

She'd been walking in the woods. She'd gotten lost. Why? Why had she been out at night alone? She couldn't remember but knew the night air had been cool and pine-scented. And she remembered the tangled, choking feeling of the woods closing around her. She had been scared, running. And then she'd ended up on the beach. That was right! She felt a little bloom of hope as that piece of the puzzle slipped into place.

She'd been standing on the beach at the lake.

And then—oh God—the bats. She remembered those. Hundreds of them. No, thousands, swirling and diving and flapping. And then the one huge black one.

It had swooped down from the giant pine tree. She'd screamed, she remembered, had instinctively curled down to the ground. She remembered smelling the cold earth close to her nose and hearing the sound of its wings beating at the air like a helicopter's blade. And then it had grabbed her. There had been hot, blue arcs of pain in her shoulders where its claws had sunk in. After that…she couldn't remember anything else. She must have passed out—maybe from the pain or maybe of fright. It must have carried her off. Carried her here.

Marion half-sobbed but then pressed her lips together. She had to be quiet. She had to keep her head straight.

If it had brought her back to its den or cave or wherever it lived, then there was a chance it was here with her now, wasn't there? Maybe it was huddled above her in the dark. Marion opened her tightly-clenched eyes and let them dart over the ceiling of the space. It must be some kind of cavern, Marion thought, wishing that she was wearing her glasses or even better, her contacts. She could see big stuff but everything was fuzzy around the edges.

Marion squinted. The space around her was washed in darkness and shadows. As far as she could tell no giant bat was sitting above her, perched like a gargoyle, and waiting for her to get up.

It was time to leave. Using her freed arm, Marion explored the other one, beneath her on the rocky ledge. The shirt's sleeve was mostly gone, ending about where her arm was covered in the foul-smelling black stuff.

Guano, she realized with disgust. Bat guano. Choking back another hysterical sob, Marion worked her trapped arm out from the goop. She brought her hand to her chest and felt more of it there. Gagging, she struggled out of the shirt and used the tails to wipe as much of the guano from her skin as she could. She crouched on the rock.

Now what?

Get out of here! Get out of here! Her brain screamed at her but she hesitated. If the bat was above her and Marion just couldn't see it she didn't want to wake it. It had been nearly three o'clock when she'd left the tent. But how long had she been here? Wouldn't she have a better chance of escaping when the bats—if they were in here—were more deeply asleep?

She would take her time. It was better to leave quietly anyway than to make a ruckus and run around panicking. If she could run. Her legs felt strange beneath her, Marion realized. Like they were dead. She lifted one and then the other. Both moved, though felt sore and stiff.

Wait.

Marion heard something. It moved in the darkness. Above her? To the side? She couldn't tell. It sounded whispery, like old leaves tumbling over the ground or dried grasses moving together. Marion rolled over and put both arms to the side of her on the big rock. She pushed upward on shaking arms. Something sharp dug into her right thigh. The glow stick! Jude had given it to her while they were sitting at the fire.

Marion dropped onto the rock on her back, panting, and fumbled in her pocket. The glow stick was supposed to be extra powerful, he'd said. She felt a sharp stab of regret in her chest but ignored it. Were you supposed to shake it and then snap it or vice versa? She couldn't remember but gave it a few halfhearted shakes and then snapped it, being careful that the plastic tube didn't slide out of her damp hands.

A bright glowing yellow filled the room. Marion gasped and hunched her body over it. Lighting the glow stick was a risk. But how could she defend herself if she couldn't see whatever was coming after her?

Slowly, cautiously, she let the light glow from under her body. She could see more clearly the rock she was on. It was coated with a wide splash of guano probably mixed with her blood. She shivered and lifted the stick with both hands clenching it tightly between her palms. She did not want to lose this thing.

Above her, the cave ceiling stood maybe forty or fifty feet overhead. Marion hesitated, then lifted both arms as high as she could. She gasped from the pain that rolled down her back and shoulders. Dizziness hit her like a wave. She swayed but maintained her balance.

Though the glow stick cast light it wasn't bright enough to hit the top of the ceiling, illuminating everything there. Marion squinted. There were lots of dark rocks above, knobby crevices, and pieces of stone jutting out here and there. And—

Marion held in a panicked scream.

Directly above her was the huge bat. It hung from delicate-looking feet from the center of the room. Its wings were leathery and blackish against the dark fur of its body. Its head was the size of a bowling ball and Marion guessed that its body was the size of a German shepherd. The scream threatened to erupt when she saw what surrounded it. Covering the ceiling like carpet, were thousands of little, furry bodies hanging upside down. They shifted and resettled their wings like one entity.

A sick, clenching feeling spread in Marion's gut as she lowered the light. What was she going to do? This could not be happening. Her head throbbed. A giant bat? Stranded in a cave? She didn't know where she was. Even if she could make it out of this cave, what then? She didn't have a weapon—not that anything less than a blowtorch and can of gasoline would take care of this many bats—she had no food or water or even another shirt other than the tank top she shivered in now.

Still, she needed to do something. Anything. Right now, she was a sitting duck, just waiting for the whole colony of them to wake up. Glancing up again, Marion saw the big one shift slightly. She froze, her heart thumped hard in her chest. Again, she clenched the glow stick in her hands, partially hiding the light. But the big bat simply adjusted its wings, refolded them, and became still again.

She had to get out of this cave. Marion swung her legs as soundlessly as possible over the end of the large stone slab closest to the ground. It was still a drop of about six feet or so. Could she make it down without waking up the bats? Or spraining her ankle?

Grimacing, Marion scooted off the ledge. Her shoulders burned like someone had dumped hot coals over them. She tried and failed to hold in a groan of pain. There was no time to see if she'd awoken the bats overhead.

Instead, Marion let gravity take over. Her body slid down the rock face, picking up speed on its way down. By the time her feet hit the rocky ground underneath, Marion was gasping. She'd tried and failed, to keep her damaged shoulders away from the stone. Now, she could feel blood running again freely over her shoulder blades, soaking the tank top underneath.

Don't look up. Just keep moving.

Marion shone the glow stick out in front of her, hunching over to see better. There were rocks and stones in all shapes and sizes everywhere. Many of them were covered in the same goopy guano. The whole place stunk of it and the black excrement made the rocks as slippery as if they were covered in algae.

Tripping, Marion caught herself, her hand coming away covered in black ooze. She felt a hysterical laugh build in her throat and choked it down.

There was a noise from overhead. She stopped in her tracks. Turning, Marion looked up.

A section of the bats shifted again simultaneously, like a wave. First, the ones closest to the far wall spread their wings, and then the next section, all the way across the ceiling. The big bat remained immobile at first, but then it too, like it was waking up, began to flex its wings. Marion stared in horror as it opened its eyes.

Then she ran.

Chapter 6

Rick Langlois

Rick moved instinctively as Jude tumbled headfirst into the big, dark space. He'd stayed to the side of the cavern, his light illuminating the sheer drop. As soon as he heard Jude coming, Rick's hands shot out. He grabbed Jude's shorts microseconds before his son fell into the abyss that yawned open in front of them.

With a hard jerk, Rick righted the boy. He didn't release his grip from Jude's canvas shorts until after his own feet were secure on the steeply pitched ground. The rocks worked against them, tried to pitch them downhill.

"Are you all right?" Rick's voice sounded too loud in the quiet cavern.

Jude was so white he nearly glowed in the darkness. He nodded. "Sorry," he said.

"It's not your fault," Rick replied. "But from now give me a few seconds lead." He put his arm around his son. "Sure you're all right?"

Jude nodded. He was shaking. Rick was too.

They stood in silence for several long moments. Rick tried to get his bearing. His flashlight was missing. He must have dropped it when he grabbed for Jude. He fumbled around the stones for a few minutes, asked Jude to help him look but all they found were rocks of all sizes and shapes.

Finally, Jude stopped and brandished the light. He gave a tired little whoop and Rick thumped him twice on the back.

"What's that smell?" Jude asked. "It stinks in here."

Rick flicked the light down toward their feet. "There's probably been some animals using it for hibernation. Listen, let's go down carefully. Stay a few feet behind me in case... well, just in case. I'll keep the light a little behind where I'm walking so you can still see. Take your time, buddy, all right?"

Rick tested the ground. It was challenging to pick a line of descent when the rocks and stones cast shadows everywhere. Jude was right. The air was dark and foul-smelling. Rick paused to flick the light around the cavern. It was a huge room, hard to believe that something so big could be underground and naturally formed. The area was like a misshapen circle and covered in boulders and stones. Far down on the floor of the cave, Rick saw a long, flat ledge. It was marbled with thick bands of black over its surface. All the rest of the stones in the space were a jumble of shapes and sizes. The shades ranged from gray to brown, to black, and many variations, from what Rick could make out.

"Do you see her?" Jude's voice was strained.

Rick shook his head. "No, not yet. Keep your eyes on your footing, buddy. We'll look around when we get down." The smell was getting worse. Rick's eyes were starting to tear up from the thick ammonia odor. He wondered how Jude was faring but didn't ask.

The leather sheath where Rick's bowie knife was strapped rubbed against the stones as he slid down them. He kept his feet out in front, catching himself from going too fast down the bigger rock faces. Jude was falling further and further behind, but Rick figured he'd catch up. And if Rick found Marion at the bottom, he wanted time to assess her condition before their son saw her. What had she been doing in here? The question circled in his brain like a June bug around a glass globe on the porch light.

"Dad?" Jude's voice was quiet. They'd both switched to whispers in the tunnel. The deeper in they got, the quieter their voices had become.

Rick stopped where he was, nearly three-quarters of the way to the bottom, and looked back over his shoulder. Jude was gripping a big rock with one hand and keeping the other over his nose and mouth. He pulled it free a moment to point at the far side of the cavern.

Rick followed his son's finger. A little light glowed, faint and yellow. It was hard to make it out with the bright beam of his flashlight. Rick flicked it off, casting them both momentarily into solid darkness. His eyes adjusted and he saw the light was moving, bobbing across the floor of the cavern.

"What is it?" Jude asked.

Rick shook his head. He wasn't sure but at that moment something else caught his attention. He sensed movement from the corner of his eye and glanced upward. Was that—

He flicked the flashlight back on. The beam bounced over rocks and a lumpy, bumpy ceiling overhead. Except there was something wrong with those rocks. They were—

"Dad!" Jude's voice was a panicked whisper. "Dad, look at all the bats!"

Jude clambered down the rocks and stones too fast. They skidded and skittered down under his feet.

"Careful," Rick said. But at that moment, Jude lost his balance. He slipped, reached out his hands, and said something unintelligible before falling behind a giant boulder. Rick swore and hauled himself back up the way he'd just come down. His heart pumped hard in his chest, a staccato beat against his ribcage.

"Jude? You all right?" he whispered. His voice was hoarse and his breath was nearly a pant now. "Jude?"

"Yeah, I'm all right," his son's voice replied. "But my foot is stuck."

Rick scrambled over the rest of the rocks between them and came to rest against the side of a massive boulder. Jude was propped against it, one foot wedged securely between the rock and another, smaller boulder nearby.

"I slipped," Jude said.

"Yeah, I saw that. Listen, buddy, we need to get you out of here. And we need to be quiet while we do it, okay?"

Jude stared. "Did you see them, Dad? Did you see the bats? There must be millions of them."

"I know. Look, can you—"

"I'm scared, Dad. What if they all fly at us? What if they bite us? I hate bats."

"Buddy—"

A cry split through the nearly silent air.

Rick and Jude looked at each other, then tried to peer around the side of the big boulder.

"What was that?" Jude asked. His eyes were huge and a worried line creased his brows.

Rick shook his head. "I don't know. Let's get you unstuck so we can get out and see."

"It could be Mom," Jude said and jerked his leg frantically.

"Dad, come on."

"Don't." He put a hand on his son's shoulder. "We've got to ease your foot out, not jerk it like that. It's just going to make it worse. We can't do anything until we get you free."

Jude gave one final jerk and then lay back and stared up at the ceiling.

A big tear rolled from each of Jude's eyes. "Hurry," he said, his thin chest heaving.

Rick heard the fear in his son's voice. He dropped into a crouch and felt around the stones again. He handed Jude the flashlight and reminded him to point it down at his foot, not the bats. Jude's hiking boot was firmly stuck between two boulders. He was lucky he hadn't broken his ankle. Rick got a hand around the boot and pulled, but it didn't budge.

He tried again and again. No luck. The boot was firmly wedged in place.

"Can you move your foot? It might be better to take your boot off until after your foot is free."

Jude tested his foot and nodded. "I can move it."

"All right." Rick bent over his son's boot, strained to untie the chunky black laces.

"Got it," he said. "Now pull."

Jude struggled but his awkward angle made it impossible. Rick reached down, grabbed his son's foot, and pulled up and sideways. It took a few seconds but finally, Jude's sock-covered foot came free of the hiking boot.

"There. Now just hold on a second..." Rick worked at the boot, wiggling it this way and that. It was easier to maneuver and manhandle now that there wasn't a foot in the way. He glanced around them, scanned for signs of movement but didn't see anything in the periphery.

Finally, the boot came loose. "Got it," he said and held the boot out to his son. Rick took a second while Jude crammed his foot back into the boot to catch his breath. As soon as Jude was done tying the laces back up, Rick flicked off the flashlight.

"Hey—"

"Just wait for a second," Rick said. He looked for the light bobbing beneath them again. But it was gone. Turning the light back on, he swept his gaze up overhead. The bats there were moving, curling and uncurling their wings. His gaze caught something else. He swallowed and blinked. Looked again.

It was still there.

Hanging dead center in the forest of bats hung one that was impossibly huge. Rick felt a wave of revulsion wash over him, mixed with disbelief. There was no way that thing could be real. And yet, as Rick watched, it unfurled giant, leathery wings.

"Dad?" Jude said, seeing the bat at the same time. His voice held a note of panic.

"Dad? Is that...is that real?"

As though hearing Jude's question the bat opened its eyes.

Jude yelled. Rick threw himself over his son as the bat let go of its hold on the ceiling and plunged downward.

Chapter 7

Marion Langlois

Marion stumbled and fell. The glow stick slipped from her greasy fingers at the same time a moan fell from her mouth. Her right knee had smashed hard into a rock. She lay there and assessed the damage.

Move, move, move! Her brain commanded.

She moved.

Reaching around the boulder closest to her, Marion climbed back to her feet. She looked around for the fluorescent light but couldn't see it. Dammit! She'd lost the only light she had.

Above there was the distinctive *flap-flap-flap* of huge wings. Flattening herself to the ground once more, Marion looked wildly over her shoulder.

It flew down from the ceiling of the cave. Marion would have yelled but was so scared her throat constricted.

Move, move, move! Her brain screamed again.

She crawled toward the wall closest to her. Was this the way to the exit? She had no idea. But if she could get to the wall, she'd follow it until she found an opening. There had to be one somewhere.

The sound of the flapping wings was slow compared to the

rat-a-tat-tat drumbeat of her heart. She shimmied up over a large boulder.

Don't look back. Do not look back. You've got to keep moving.

Marion couldn't help it. She looked back. The bat was to her left. It was getting closer.

Move, move—The little voice in her mind was replaced when a strange tremor hit her body. It was almost like an electrical shock but not as painful. For a second, Marion couldn't breathe. Then it felt like her body was slowing down even though her brain screamed at her to go faster. She had to get away from it. Had to put more distance between herself and those impossibly big wings. The feeling that had slammed into her faded quickly. The bat hissed; the sound cut through the hushed quiet of the cavern like a saw.

Marion hauled herself to the top of a nearby boulder, then half slid, half skidded down the other side. Her foot—the one still encased in a canvas shoe—hit a smooth stone. She flattened herself to the ground again.

And waited.

She was certain any second she'd feel the knife-like claws dig into her back and shoulders again. If only she'd had her jackknife in her pocket. Or anything else she could use as a weapon. She hadn't thought she'd need them when she'd left the tent to go to the bathroom.

The bat's wings sounded like they were moving further away. Marion held her breath and peeked out from her hiding spot. She was crouched low in a small crevice, her arms thrown over her head in a pathetic attempt at self-protection.

It was true. The bat flew away from her. Up and toward the left.

Why? Why would it leave her now? Surely it could have

flattened its body down, made it into this pathetic hiding spot with ease.

Marion took advantage of the unexpected freedom to look around the cavern better. She'd been so focused on escape and making it to a wall that she hadn't paid much attention to the rest of the huge room of stone. It was hard to make things out in the dimness. If only she hadn't lost that glow stick…but wait. What was that?

There was a light above her. At about ten o'clock. She could see it. But why would there be a light down here?

"Dad!" a yell. "Dad, do something!"

Jude. Marion's heart fluttered once extra-fast in her chest as her stomach dropped like she was on a rollercoaster. They'd found her, come to save her. And now—

Marion was about to call out when the light bobbed. It moved frantically, like an angry bee. Then Rick shouted. Marion couldn't make out what he'd said. The light bounced frantically. Marion saw the huge bat circling the light. She stood unmoving, not even able to blink. Fear clutched at her chest, smothered her cry.

The light bobbed a final time and winked out. Rick yelled again, a cry of pain.

The sound brought Marion out of her stupor. She scrambled over the rocks and stones, ignoring the pain as they bit into her palms. Climbing a boulder, she lost her footing and slid halfway back down, then climbed up again. The rocks were slick and greasy under her hands. More than once she banged a limb. She ignored all the pain and focused on where she'd seen the light. Where she'd heard her husband and son's voices.

There was another yell. She was half frantic and half relieved. At least he was still able to call out, she thought.

Then another noise filled the space. It was like wind rushing through the cavern. Heavy, strong wind, like you heard when a thunderstorm was just about to start. There was a movement in the corner of her eye. She looked up.

Bats—hundreds of them, tons of them—were flying around the cavern in erratic waves. Marion wanted to scream but was too breathless. She kept climbing.

Jude. Rick. Jude. Rick.

She had to get to them. She had to.

Marion's palms slipped off the sharp edge of a big rock she'd been scaling. She felt the skin tear away but kept climbing.

The bats continued to circle. They made strange, dizzying loops around the room. The feeling she'd had, like an electrical pulse, got stronger. Now, it felt like the air all around her was charged. She had to be close.

Where was the giant bat? She couldn't waste precious seconds looking. It felt like she'd been climbing for hours, for days. She was panting and sweating and crying all at the same time. She wiped her face on the inside of her bare arm and assessed her location.

She could see the light just ahead, a few yards. She was close. Much closer than she had been minutes ago. But would she get to Rick in time? The light was on the ground. It pointed upward into the swirl of bats flying helter-skelter overhead. Marion couldn't see Rick or Jude. Where were they? Had the giant bat taken one of them? Both?

Jude screamed.

Marion launched herself over another big stone. Something warm oozed under her bare foot. She scrambled toward her son. She tried to call out but had no breath to do it.

"Jude! Run!" Rick's voice boomed from just ahead and to

her left.

"Dad?"

Almost there.

Rick screamed.

"Dad!"

A strange whooshing sound filled the cavern and then a pulse of sonar so powerful that Marion froze mid-reach. She was frozen, paralyzed. After a few seconds, it began to fade. She craned her neck toward her family.

The giant bat had Rick in its talons. They were closed over his lower torso and leg. Blood already darkened his pants. A low moaning sound came from the back of Marion's throat. The big bat hissed. The smaller ones—hundreds of them—circled closer and closer.

The bat adjusted its grip, steadied its wings before starting to flap them again. Rick cried out as the bat's claws dug deeper into his flesh.

Marion launched herself toward the boulder in front of her. She was close. Nearly there.

A rock flew out of the darkness. It hit the big bat's right wing and bounced off.

"Hey, you stupid ugly jerk. Let go!"

The bat juddered then tightened its claws over its prey. Rick cried out again.

"Jude...run," Rick moaned.

Chapter 8

Jude Langlois

Snot and tears ran down Jude's face. He heard his father yell at him to run but his feet felt stuck to the ground. He stared at the huge bat—so big!—and felt another sob in his throat. Peyton would never believe him...if he ever saw Peyton again.

Something clattered over the rocks behind him. He turned, dread filling his belly like his grandmother's brick-like fruit-cake. What would he see? Another Godzilla-sized bat perched on a nearby boulder, waiting to grab him, too?

Instead, he saw a figure covered in mud. It climbed over a boulder and slid down toward him. It was a woman he realized. It was—

"Mom?"

"Jude, Jude." She grabbed him and wrapped her arms around him. He clung to her, felt her shoulders shaking under his hands. Her arms felt strong and familiar, though she reeked. Too quickly, she pushed him away from her, fingers biting into his upper arms.

"We've got to help your father." She looked into his face, tears tracking crooked lines down her dirty face. He'd never

49

seen his mother dirty before. Even when she came in from gardening, she always looked clean. It was stupid, but he hadn't even realized she could get dirty. Or smelly. Or—

"Listen, baby, this is what we're going to do." She hurriedly told him her plan. It sounded impossible to Jude and he wanted to tell her all the reasons it wouldn't work. But when he looked at his father, Jude only nodded and told her he understood.

Mom motioned to Jude to follow her. Together, they eased closer to where the giant bat had Dad pinned to the ground. His father moaned quietly and lay very, very still. Blood dripped in rivers out of the places where the bat's claws dug into Dad's skin. He had an ugly red cut on his forehead and more blood was smeared there. Jude's mouth filled with spit like it did before he threw up.

"Ready?" Mom asked.

Jude nodded and made himself swallow again and again. He crouched and grabbed some rocks.

"Hey, hey you big stupid bat!" Jude was partially hidden behind a large boulder in a small crevice. His voice was too quiet at first and shook with tears. He coughed, tried again.

"Stupid thing!" he yelled and like Mom had said to, chucked a few small rocks at it. The bat swiveled its big head, looking in their direction.

Or Jude's direction. Mom was nowhere in sight.

The cloud of bats overhead started to make tighter and tighter circles around Dad. They flew close to him. Dipped down and—were they biting him? His father groaned, then cried out when two swarmed around his exposed neck. Anger like lava flowed through Jude. He took another handful of rocks and threw them toward the cloud of circling bats. He wanted to get the two near Dad but was afraid he'd hit him

50

instead.

Again and again, he yelled, throwing more stones, not even bothering to aim. He just needed to distract them long enough...

Jude saw his mother, half-blended in with the dark stones. She crept up behind the big bat.

Closer. Closer.

She was within a few feet of the giant bat's head now. Jude bit his lips together so hard they went numb. Mom slipped her hand around Dad's legs from the back, reached up, and pulled the long bowie knife free.

Dad groaned. The big bat was looking toward Jude.

Do something, stupid, he thought. He opened his mouth and yelled as loud as he could. Found stones and cracked them against each other, the sound ringing out and echoing around the cavern.

The bat still watched him. As it did, it unfurled its long, leathery-looking wings. A strange hissing noise came from its gray face and it bared its teeth. They were sharp and jagged looking. Jude froze, a stone in his hand.

The bat flapped its wings, once, twice three times.

It jutted its head forward, toward Jude.

Jude gasped. Fear, like a smothering blanket, fell over him. It was coming for him. The bat was coming.

Warm wetness ran down his leg.

The bat released its hold on his father and started to walk strangely, disjointedly, using the triangular fold of its wings like extra feet. Jude knew he should run—that's what Mom had told him to do—but he couldn't move. He stared in horrified fascination as the big bat drew closer. Weird jolts—almost like when he touched his grandparents' electric fence—ran through his body.

It was getting closer.

Too close.

There was a little whimpering sound and then Jude realized it was coming from him. He should do something—grab a rock or run for cover—but he couldn't move. The pulses were coming faster and stronger. He was paralyzed. The pulses rocked through his body. He felt like a bug trapped in a bug zapper, being stunned over and over again.

The bat's mouth was still open. Its teeth were very white. Jude heard himself yell and then another strong jolt zinged through his body. The other bats circled faster and tighter. The cavern was full of the sound of wings now and strange squeaks that came from the small bats. Jude felt his body shaking but couldn't stop it. It was like when he came in after too long sledding and couldn't stop shivering.

The bat raised its head, spread out its enormous wings.

Jude closed his eyes.

His mother yelled, half-scream and half-hyena screech.

Jude opened his eyes. A sharp, silver wedge appeared in the giant bat's chest. It screeched—a wail so loud that Jude's ears immediately rang and wouldn't stop. The bat jerked once, twice, three times. Then it crumpled to the ground. His mother stood behind it. She put a foot on the bat's back and pulled out the blade, then drove it in again and again and again, grunting every time.

She slumped over the bat for a second, before getting to her feet. She wobbled, then rushed to Jude's side. She hugged him tightly. He couldn't move his arms but felt his body starting to come to life again.

"Are you okay?" She patted him—shoulders, arms, torso.

"Jude, can you hear me? Are you okay?"

"Mom?" A little line of drool came out of his mouth. He reached up with a shaky, strange-feeling hand and wiped it off.

"Oh, thank God. You're okay. You're okay." She repeated this over and over like she needed to convince them both. Finally, she gave him a hard squeeze.

"You did such a good job, baby. Now we've got to hurry and get Dad out of here."

Jude nodded. Then, "Mom, I peed my pants."

"It's okay. Come with me."

She kissed the top of his head and held out a hand, the one that wasn't covered in blood. Jude grabbed it.

***

It took a long time to get out of the cavern. Jude's mother propped up one side of Dad and he helped hold up his other side. His father didn't talk much, mostly moaned. Mom had used the rest of her ratty shirt to tie around Dad's leg, where most of the blood was coming from. She said once they were outside she could get the rest of him bandaged up.

They found the tunnel where Jude and his father had come in and, with lots of pushing and pulling, managed to get Dad through the narrow space. Their packs were on the other side and Mom almost started crying again when she saw them.

Strangely, the smaller bats had all flown away after the big one had been killed. Jude thought about *The Wizard of Oz* and wondered if the bats—like the flying monkeys—had been under some kind of evil spell. He hoped so and that they were long gone, maybe in another state by now.

It felt like hours before they finally made it out of the tunnel. Finally, they laid down under a big pine tree downhill from the cavern's entrance. Jude hoped he'd never see another cave or bat as long as he lived. He drank big gulps of water even though Mom said to take it slow and then felt sick to his stomach.

When it felt better, he found clean pants in his backpack and changed. Mom had pulled out the first aid kit and cleaned out Dad's wounds, applying gross-smelling ointment and wrapping everything up in bright-white bandages.

"Have something to eat, honey," Mom told him as she started to work on her own feet and hands. They were filthy, covered in mud, and—Jude didn't want to know what else—and there was caked blood all over her. She looked like someone who'd survived the zombie apocalypse...barely.

Jude leaned back against the tree, keeping an eye on the big cavern. It was almost nighttime.

"Are we going to have to sleep out here?"

"What?" Mom asked, her voice distracted.

"Are we going to have to sleep out here, in the woods?"

"Um, yes. Probably, baby."

Jude swallowed hard. The apple he'd just eaten felt like it was stuck in his throat. He didn't even like apples—or fruit—but right now he'd eat anything. He rummaged in his pack and pulled out a stick of jerky and chewed on it.

Even though the bats had disappeared, he still almost expected to see them come pouring out of the cavern. Dad moaned and then moved around.

"Don't, hon." Mom left her bandaging half undone and scooted close to Dad's head. She put a hand on his head, smoothed a hand over the skin that was showing there.

"Can you drink anything? I have ibuprofen if you can swallow them."

Dad nodded slowly. "Yes," he said. His voice was so weak Jude barely heard it.

"Good," Mom said. She was smiling as she rummaged through the bag. Seconds later, she brought out a shiny packet and a water bottle. She helped Dad hold his head up and gave him the pills, then helped him drink. Water spilled down the side of his mouth and she wiped it away with the back of her hand. She dipped her face closer to Dad's and talked to him too quietly for Jude to hear.

A warm glow spread in Jude's belly. Here they were, in the middle of nowhere, almost killed by psycho bats and he felt happy. He shook his head and took another bite of jerky. It had been a long time since he'd seen his parents get along. It had been a long time since they'd taken care of each other. Jude wasn't sure but he thought that must be an important part of being married. Not that he'd ever find out. Peyton and Rebecca were boyfriend and girlfriend but the thought of that made Jude want to puke. Girls were gross…mostly because they were so weird.

"…should we?" Dad whispered, his voice rough like sandpaper.

"I've been thinking about it," Mom replied. "Let's wait until morning."

Jude shivered. He didn't want to stay here in the woods. And he especially didn't want to stay outside of this bat cave. He was never watching *Batman* again, that was for sure. Thinking about the movie made Jude think of something though. Superheroes. Would Iron Man, his favorite, sit around waiting to get attacked? Would he have let his parents do all

55

the hard work while he screamed and peed his pants?

Shame washed over Jude hot and sticky. He was a loser. But maybe he could change that. If he went back to camp, he could get help. There were other campers somewhere in the campground, even if they couldn't see them through the woods that separated their sites. He could find someone and ask them to go get help—get the ranger or the police or a helicopter—and rescue his parents.

It was a good idea. Jude knew he could find the way back. Well, he was pretty sure. It would be easier with a GPS but those didn't work here. Too much tree cover, his father had said. Or was it clouds? Anyway, imagine what Peyton would say when Jude told him what he'd done.

"Yeah, I saved my parents. But you know," Jude would shrug his shoulders, "it's no big deal."

Dad closed his eyes and seemed to sleep. Mom went back to her bandaging. Jude could see the back of her shoulders—they looked disgusting, like steaks from the grocery store. He walked over to her.

"Mom?"

"Mmmhmm?" she mumbled. She closed her eyes and pressed her lips together as she reached over her back and tried to spread some of the first-aid cream on herself.

"I was thinking maybe I could go get help. Find one of the other campers or the ranger and ask them to—"

Mom gasped and lowered her hands. Her face was really white. "What? No. That's too dangerous. We'll figure something out in the morning. For right now, we need to get some rest. Okay, honey?"

Jude felt deflated.

"There is something you could do to help though. Would

you mind—I know it's gross—but would you mind spreading some of this on the lower parts of my back? I can't reach and I don't want an infection to set in."

Jude swallowed. He did not want to touch his mother's back. Just looking at it was making his stomach feel wiggly like it was full of jelly.

His mother saw his face. "It's okay, baby. I'll figure something out."

"No. I can do it." He grabbed the tube from his mother's hand before he changed his mind. Her tank top was torn and he could see where the claws from the bat had ripped through the cloth. He breathed out of his mouth and smeared some of the lotion around on any parts of her skin that were red or bloody looking. He heard her gasp once when he spread it around a really deep cut.

"Sorry," he said.

"It's fine. It's okay. Please get as many as you can."

Finally, after every spot he could see was coated, he handed the tube back to her.

"Thanks. Let's wash our hands." She was shaking when she stood up.

"Do you want to hold onto me?" he asked. But she just smiled and shook her head.

They found a little packet of antibacterial wipes in the pack and wiped their hands until they were finally clean. Jude handed her a water bottle he found in the pack and she took several slow sips.

"We'll make a temporary camp for tonight and then first thing tomorrow, we'll leave, okay?" she said.

Jude nodded. They put down extra clothes on the ground to make a sleeping pad and then drew up close to Dad. Mom fell asleep before Jude, her mouth was partially open. Jude kept an eye on the mouth of the cavern. It was the last thing he saw before he fell into a deep, dreamless sleep.

***

When Jude woke up the sky had turned from dark to pearly-gray. It was morning—early, early morning. He yawned, trying to remember where he was and what had happened. When he did, he glanced over at his parents. Both were still sleeping. His mother was on her side, her raw-looking back exposed to the air. A few mosquitoes were taking advantage of the situation and Jude waved a hand over them. Dad moaned every few breaths quietly and shifted around.

Jude looked at the sky again. Quietly he got up and found a little pad of paper and stubby pencil in his emergency kit. Mom and him had put it together weeks before this trip. There was a compass, a tinfoil-looking blanket that Mom had spread over Dad last night, waterproof matches, a jackknife, bug spray, sunscreen, an extra filter for his water bottle, and some other stuff he didn't recognize.

He wrote a quick note and left it on the clothes he'd been laying on. Dad had tried to teach him how to use a compass but Jude didn't understand how it worked. All the numbers on the dial confused him. Still, he pulled it out and squinted at it in the near-dark. The red arrow pointed north when he aimed it at the cave. And then when he turned in the other direction, the one him and Dad had come from, it said south. Well, that was easy. All he had to do was keep going south. He'd find the campground, find the ranger and get help.

Satisfied with the plan, Jude checked his pack. He took some

58

granola bars, two oranges and left the rest of the bars and fruit along with an extra water bottle for his parents. He also left most of the extra clothes. It was chilly now, so he'd kept on his sweatshirt, but was sure that would be enough. The rest of the Emergency Kit he'd take with him. Who knew what he'd need on this adventure?

"See you soon, guys," he whispered. Then he pulled on his pack and started walking.

Chapter 9

Rick Langlois

Rick was having the weirdest dreams of his life. There was a singing clown that kept dancing around, weaving into and out of his peripheral vision. A giant alligator opened its mouth wide and one of Rick's favorite country songs came out of its throat. And he could hear Marion's voice calling to him but he was in the ocean and the waves kept bobbing up and down in front of his face so that he couldn't find her.

He shifted on the uncomfortable bed. They needed a new mattress…or had he fallen out? Maybe he was laying on the floor. Rick tried to open his eyes but they felt glued shut. He was hot—too hot—but when he pushed the blankets off, they reappeared. They were choking him, smothering him.

And then he was shivering, so cold that his teeth chattered. He felt something soft and dry on his forehead, then it moved away.

"Rick." It was Marion's voice. He was back in the sea though, and couldn't find her in the bobbing, churning waves.

"Rick?" Her voice was coming from the alligator's mouth now. Rick moved closer, peering in for a better look. The gator had huge, sharp-looking teeth that were yellowed. Rick's throat was dry. He thought *this is a dumb idea* as he watched himself put his hand into the big alligator's mouth. But instead of the teeth slamming shut on his arm, it turned and clamped onto his upper thigh. Rick howled as pain exploded there. Stars shot off around his head.

He heard Marion whisper, "Rick? Rick, you're going to be okay."

Then everything went black.

Chapter 10

Marion Langlois

Something was wrong. Marion knew as soon as she opened her eyes. She propped herself up on an elbow, wiped the gritty sleep from her eyes, and looked around. The forest was noisy. The earliest of the birds were squabbling and squawking and nearby a woodpecker drilled on a tree.

Marion hurt. This must be what it felt like to wake up after you've been run over, she thought. Everything ached, from her head to her toes. Her back and shoulders hurt worst of all. The throbbing in her head came in a close second though. She ran her fingers over her scalp. She'd been so focused on Rick last night and getting antibacterial on her back that she'd forgotten to check her head. She'd passed out when the bat had taken her and didn't know how she'd gotten from the lake to the cavern. A large lump on the back of her head told her that she'd been dropped onto the big stone she'd woken up on. Crusted blood around the lump was minimal and Marion didn't bother trying to get it out of her hair.

She glanced around groggily. Rick was shaking under the mylar blanket. The spot next to her where Jude had slept was empty.

"Jude?" she called out in a loud whisper, trying not to wake Rick. "Jude, where are you?"

No answer except from the woodpecker which knocked again in rapid-fire. He must have gone to the bathroom further out in the trees.

"Rick?" She moved to her husband's side and looked down at him. His face was so white she could easily see the light blue veins under his skin. She put a hand to his forehead and found it damp and very hot.

Not good.

She pushed the blanket off of him and he moaned. He reached feebly out for it but Marion tucked it under her knees while she rolled him gently to his good side. The bat's claws had torn a deep gash in Rick's leg but must have missed the artery. He'd lost a lot of blood—most of it in the cavern—and she needed to make sure that it hadn't restarted bleeding during the night. She pulled the tape from one side of the bandage free and took a cursory glance. The white gauze pad was soaked. Fresh blood trickled from the wound. The slash was jagged and red, with tattered edges where the bat's talons had sliced through Rick's skin. All around the gouge, the skin was red and inflamed-looking.

Marion bit her lip and pulled the rest of the bandage free as gently as she could. Still, it took a lot of Rick's hair with it and he moaned again.

"Sorry," she said. "I'm so sorry. I'm going to put a fresh bandage on and get this feeling better, okay?"

Rick didn't answer.

Marion spent the next ten minutes alternately yelling for Jude and rewrapping all of Rick's bandages. She was sweating by the end and felt light-headed. She walked on her knees over to where she and Jude had made makeshift beds.

Where was he? Even if he'd gone to the bathroom, he should have been back by now. An itchy creeping fear ran along the back of her neck.

"Jude?" she called out again, but again there was no answer.

Marion looked at her feet. The one without a shoe was cut in several places on the arch and around the heel. She should get those cleaned out, something else she hadn't bothered with last night.

Last night.

Had it been only hours ago? Everything felt like it had happened in slow motion. She could barely remember packing for the trip. She'd been stressed out, she remembered that. Worried that they'd forget something important. That they'd be inconvenienced.

She snorted out a laugh. When she thought of how close they'd come to dying—she shivered. She couldn't believe it. Still. Even all these hours later. And when they got out of here, if they got out of here, who would ever believe the crazy story? A giant bat and a swarm of other blood-thirsty ones…it was too unreal to be true.

"Jude?" Marion called again. Another wave of dizziness washed over her and she put her hand down. Something crinkled underneath it. Marion squinted and picked up a piece of paper. It stuck out from underneath a couple of oranges and a little pile of granola bars.

Mom and Dad,

Going to get help. Back soon.

Love you,
Jude

No. No, no, no, no, no.

Marion sank back on her heels, read the note again, and then cried aloud, "No!"

Oh, why would he…but she didn't even finish the thought. She knew why: he wanted to save them. Jude probably thought he had the best chance of finding help. Marion grimaced. She hated the thought of her son out in these woods all alone. But could he be right?

She could barely walk and even if she could, how would they get Rick out of here? She wasn't strong enough to carry him. And there's no way she'd leave him. If Jude had been here, maybe he could have stayed with his father while she went for help. She smiled wryly. Not that she'd be much better in the woods than her son.

But no. They should be together. It was dangerous out there, alone. Her stomach twisted unpleasantly. What if he got lost? What if a wild animal attacked him? Jude didn't know enough about maps or the outdoors to be safe by himself in the woods. Rick had tried to teach him how to use a compass—she checked the Emergency Kit and saw it was gone—but she wasn't confident Jude had understood. As a kid, Rick probably could have made it safely back to their camp and alerted the authorities. He'd started hunting when he was five with his father and older brothers. But not Jude. She tried to think: what skills would their son have? He'd been part of the local Cub Scout troop when he was younger, something Rick had encouraged him to take part in before he'd taken over the garage. It had only lasted about a year, but maybe some of that knowledge would stick.

Rick groaned again and Marion roused herself, found more ibuprofen—there were only six left—and the water bottle.

"Here, honey," she said and put a hand around Rick's face. "Try to get these down."

Some of the water spilled, soaking Rick's already damp shirt and he moaned more loudly and turned away before she could get the pills into his mouth. His jaws were clenched together so hard she'd barely gotten any of the water into his mouth. He had a fever. What was the best thing to do? Keep him as comfortable as possible until help arrived.

Help. The thought brought a mirthless chuckle.

Oh God...please, please let Jude be all right.

Rick had to have this medicine. It was the only hope they had of fighting off the fever. Marion ground the ibuprofen tablets to powder between two small stones and diluted them in the water bottle cap. She held Rick's chin in one hand and forced the milky-looking water into Rick's mouth. Some of it sprayed out when he coughed in her face, but most of it went down his throat. She wiped off her face and looked around them. What could she use here to make Rick more comfortable and to raise the alarm when and if help did come looking for them?

They were situated a way away from the cavern, though not as far as Marion would like. She'd meant to watch for the remaining bat colony to come out last night but had fallen asleep before she'd had a chance to see anything. Now, she assessed the location.

They were lying under a very large pine tree. Trees were all over the place here, with little light getting through the thick canopy overhead. That wasn't good. If there was a rescue attempt at some point, a helicopter wouldn't see them under here. Still, the thought of being out in the open, exposed to the sun and wind and wild animals didn't sound good either. The tree did provide shelter. If it rained it would be better than nothing.

So, what could she do? Around the thick tangle of trees were…more trees. Further away, on the left side of the cavern was a fairly open area. Maybe she could create a fire to signal for help. She got up, limped out from under the pine tree for a better look. The cavern itself was very high—it likely looked like a gigantic boulder or small hill from the air. Maybe if she could put something up there—something brightly colored—that would help draw attention. But what? They hadn't packed fluorescent paint. Still, there must be something.

Excitement swept over her. *Yes.* She would do both of those things. And then if Rick got better…

No.

She shoved the thoughts aside. He would get better. Jude would find help. They would be rescued. She refused to think otherwise.

Right now, she had work to do. And none of it was going to easy without a shoe and in the tattered rag of a tank top she wore. Marion dug through the extra clothes lying on the ground and found one of Rick's T-shirts. She put it to one side and kept looking. There were a few other shirts, two extra pairs of underwear, a pair of Jude's extra canvas hiking pants, two pairs of rolled-up socks, and…that was it. Still. It was a good assortment. She was thankful Rick had had the good sense to grab packs before they'd come looking for her. She was glad too, that he always carried the bowie knife whenever they went into the woods.

"You never know," he'd say every time she'd asked incredulously if he "really needed to bring that knife?".

"Never know when it might come in handy." He'd grin and give Jude a wink. Marion had usually just rolled her eyes. Now she felt her cheeks redden. If he hadn't had the knife last night…She checked for the bowie knife now, knowing she'd feel relieved when it was close by. It hadn't been in the leather sheath that Rick had strapped to his leg. Marion had unfastened that last night and it lay empty near his makeshift bed. It wasn't mixed in with any of the items she'd pulled from the pack. Had it fallen onto the grass? Had one of them been sleeping on it? She started to look but even as she did a sick feeling enveloped her stomach. She couldn't remember seeing the knife after she'd killed the bat.

She remembered the sickening sensation and the awful crunching noises when she'd plunged the knife in. She remembered the smell—even over the ammonia-scented air—of blood and other bodily fluids that the bat had sprayed. But she couldn't remember seeing the knife after that.

Realization dawned like a spray of icy-cold water.

It had to be here. It couldn't *not* be here, Marion thought with dizzying panic.

But she knew. Even as she frantically searched through the contents of the backpack strewn around the makeshift campsite, she knew.

It was still in the cave.

Marion had been in such a hurry to get Rick and Jude out to safety that she'd left their only weapon behind. She squeezed her forehead with both hands and held in a sob of frustration. *Get it together,* she thought. Anger at herself and her stupidity rose hot and salty in her chest. The knife was in there and they were out here.

That was the truth and she'd have to deal with it.

Gathering the clothes up, she placed the bundle on a dry log nearby. She kept out one pair of socks and canvas pants. As she tore strips of the canvas, she ate half of a granola bar. She also peeled an orange, ate half of that, and dribbled most of the juice from the other half into Rick's mouth. He was still just as hot but he wasn't moaning as frequently. She hoped it meant he was more comfortable.

Marion pulled off her tattered remaining canvas shoe and was about to throw it into the forest, but thought better of it. It might come in useful for something. She remembered a survival show she'd watched with Rick once when Jude had been a baby. Experts would run through different scenarios and grade participants on whether they'd made the right choices or not. One of the kernels of advice they'd given was to save everything. Every bit of material, every scrap of worthless junk. You never knew when it might come in handy, the experts had said over and over.

So, Marion set aside the shoe. She put clean socks on her feet after she'd cleaned them off and dried them and applied so many Band-Aids she looked ridiculous. Then she wrapped her feet with the canvas from Jude's pants. It took a few failed attempts to get the material to lie smoothly but she finally got it.

When she was finished, Marion put her feet out in front of her and grinned. They weren't the cutest shoes she'd ever worn but they were certainly the ones she was most grateful for.

She stood up. The next part wouldn't be fun. With

agonizingly slow movements, Marion peeled the remainder of her blood-soaked, tattered tank top off and threw it on the ground under one of the nearby trees. Her eyes teared up as the wounds reopened on her back and along her shoulders. She gasped a little as she smeared another thin layer of antibacterial cream over all the parts she could reach. It wasn't great, but better than nothing. At least, she hoped so. She tried not to think about flies getting to the open wounds and laying eggs. Marion slipped into a fresh T-shirt of Rick's and knotted it around her waist. There. If not presentable, at least she felt more capable. And sort of human again.

Marion dug through Rick's pack to see if there was anything she'd missed the first time around. In addition to the clothes, he had a Ziplock bag full of her homemade trail cookies, a small tin with fishing lures, sunscreen, bug spray, and at the very bottom his cell phone. Marion grabbed it eagerly. There wasn't supposed to be cell signal out here, but what if...?

She pushed the on button and waited. No bars. She called 911 anyway, just in case, but there was just dead air. Sighing, she put the phone into her pocket. Maybe if she could get up higher, away from the trees...

Checking Jude's Emergency Kit one more time, Marion noted that he'd left behind a whistle, all the extra batteries for his walkie-talkies—which Marion had last seen in the tent—and a bright orange poncho still enclosed in its plastic case.

Perfect! Marion grabbed the poncho and inspected it. This could work on top of the cavern. She could spread it out on the ground and weigh it down with rocks. When the plane or helicopter came looking, they'd see this immediately. A feeling of relief washed through her as she grabbed the poncho. After checking on Rick one more time, she headed for the cavern. There was so much to do. After this, she'd need to build a fire, clean Rick's wounds out again, and try to get some more liquids into him. She wished they had the little camp stove and a way to boil water. She pushed away the thought of hot coffee and soup and concentrated on the slope ahead of her.

The climb up the side of the cavern was tricky, especially with Marion's makeshift shoes. Though she'd wrapped her feet well, the canvas wasn't anywhere near as sturdy as rubber or leather. She inhaled sharply as a particularly jagged rock bit into the bottom of her right foot. Pausing, Marion looked down to check her progress. And groaned. She was only a third of the way to the top.

Readjusting the poncho in her waistband to make it more secure, Marion started climbing again. She tried to block out the thoughts of all the things that could go wrong, and of Jude alone in the woods, with the images of their cozy little home. How many times in the past few years had she longed for something else, something bigger and more modern? How many times had she felt envious when her friends traveled with their families? But Rick had said that it wasn't a good time to move or renovate. And travel—anything further than a long weekend—was out of the question right now. They needed the money for the garage, to make sure things there were secure.

"He is a hard worker, I'm not saying that," Marion's mother had said more than once when Rick and Marion were dating. "But are you certain that he's the best choice for you?"

A rock bit into Marion's hand and she welcomed the pain. At least it put things into perspective. Here she was, pampered little rich girl-turned-middle-class wife and mother scaling the side of a rocky mountain. She nearly laughed. What would Mother think about this?

Marion climbed for another fifteen minutes and finally reached the top of the cavern. Here, the ground was littered with stones, but not as jagged and irregularly spaced as inside the cavern. Marion quickly got her bearings and spread the bright poncho out fully. Then she took rocks—as big as she could carry—and weighed down the edges all the way around. When she was done, she sat on a big stone overlooking their makeshift camp, breathing hard. Sweat trickled down her back and stung the open skin. She wished she'd brought a water bottle.

She looked over the edge. Rick's mylar blanket was far below along with an accumulation of supplies spread all over the ground. She'd need to clean things up when she got back, once she got a fire going. Keeping what little supplies they had safe and usable was important. And anyway, there was—

A funny sound filled the suddenly-still air. Why had all the birds stopped chattering? She glanced around. They were still there, in the trees, but were silently flying from branch to branch. None of them tweeted and none of them dropped out of the trees and down to the ground to pick at worms or seeds. Marion listened harder. What had she heard exactly?

A faint huffing sound. Panting, like their old dog, Beanie, after Marion had walked him—back when he'd been alive and had loved to accompany her. She strained her eyes, looking around cautiously at the woods beyond Rick and their camp.

Nothing.

Nothing moved. Just the leaves. She felt the slight breeze that pushed them. She shrugged, got to her feet. She would love to rest longer but she did want to get the fire—

And then she heard it again. This time, the barely-audible panting sound was accompanied by the rustle of undergrowth. Marion scanned the perimeter.

On the edge of the woods, about one-quarter of the way around the clearing, she saw a flash of gray. Then another of brownish white. What was it? Marion squinted hard and raised her hand to shield her eyes. The leaves and thick undergrowth blocked her view. She racked her brain, trying to think of wild animals with fur in Vermont. Pine martens, raccoons, opossum...but the animals below her were much bigger...

Marion started downhill.

Huh, huh, huh, huh. The panting was louder. Then she heard a growl. One yipped. Then another. A third howled an eerie, ethereal sound that made the hair on Marion's arms and neck stand on end.

Coyotes.

A pack of them.

They jittered in and out of the trees, dancing toward the makeshift camp, then pausing to sniff the air.

Then the biggest one—the gray one Marion had seen first—began trotting directly toward Rick.

Chapter 11

Jude Langlois

Jude's stomach growled loudly. He put a hand there and felt it move underneath his fingers. He'd brought a few bars and two oranges. But he'd eaten one bar and an orange and didn't think it was a good idea to eat any more right now. Even though he was starving, he should save some for later. He doubted he'd need them, would probably be back to the campground any minute. But still, it was a good idea to keep them for later, just in case.

He wondered what his parents were doing now. Was Dad better? Was Mom worrying about Jude? He snorted. Of course, she was. That's what Mom did. He tripped over a root and caught himself on a nearby sapling. When he pulled his hand away it smelled like Christmas. He looked down at the sticky, gummy substance on his palm and fingers. Pine sap. He sniffed it again and grinned.

This was scary, but it was also pretty sic. He'd spent the last hour or so imagining the story he'd tell Peyton and his other friends at school. He'd pictured the hero's welcome he'd receive. Maybe the town would even have a parade in his honor. It could happen. They'd had one for Mickey Reeves when he'd come back from Afghanistan. Sure, he'd been like a war veteran. But Jude was saving lives here too.

Jude paused and leaned against a tree. It was a little cooler here in the shade. He wished he'd thought to bring his baseball hat. It would feel good to block out the blinding hot rays. They'd been learning about the solar system in school and this last unit had been on the sun. It was made up of five elements, Jude remembered: hydrogen, helium, carbon, nitrogen, and...what was the other one? He thought about it for a minute, sipped a little water, and then started walking again. Hydrogen, helium, carbon...

Something in the woods to the far right rattled tree branches. Jude stopped. A squirrel? He craned his head to see more clearly but the thick leaves overhead blocked his view. He shrugged and walked on, but glanced back every couple of feet. He didn't hear anything else and after several minutes, started to whistle. He glanced at the compass. It was still pointing south, though the little arrow had moved slightly to the east, too. Jude corrected his path until the arrow was pointing directly toward the "s" again.

Behind him came the sound of rustling leaves. Even though the grass here was tall, under that was a carpet of old leaves from last season. Something was moving through those. But what? There was a big log ahead, caught on another tree. It offered a place to get up off the ground. Jude ran to it and scrambled up, the punky, wet wood crumbling under his palms. Heaving himself upward, he lay on the log on his belly, then got into a sitting position. Then he stood. He didn't like the feeling of his legs dangling underneath him in the thick brush.

The thing—whatever it was—wasn't moving. Jude's heartbeat pounded loudly in his ears, too loudly for him to tell if the thing was still following him. He watched the grass and the branches on the shorter bushes. They moved. But Jude couldn't tell if it was because something was coming this way or if it was just the breeze moving them.

The lowest branches on the tree shook a little. A bead of sweat ran down Jude's cheek and he wiped it away, still watching the undergrowth intently.

"There's all kinds of stuff in those wood," Peyton had told him.

"I thought you said a giant bat lived there?" Jude had asked.

"Sure. But that's not the only thing."

Jude had snorted. "Well, what else then? A Bigfoot? A werewolf?"

Peyton had shaken his head. "Nah. But my brother said there are snakes and wolves. And mountain lions. Lots of them."

Jude had punched Peyton in the arm and laughed, then they'd hurriedly stuffed the remainder of their lunches into their boxes so they could get out on the playground first.

Could there be snakes and wolves here? And mountain lions? Jude had learned about mountain lions in school last year. There weren't any left in Vermont. At least, that's what the research said. But Jude's class had interviewed people in their community and one or two had said that they'd seen the big cats in the past few years. Jude shivered. His skin felt clammy despite the heat.

He remembered something else he'd learned about mountain lions: they were so quiet that you didn't even know they were in the woods with you. Until it was too late. The brush trembled again, then was still. Jude counted. One, two, three, four, five, six, seven...one branch shook, then another.

76

Jude's heartbeat pounded even faster. He wished Peyton were here with him now. Or that his parents were. Or that he wasn't in these woods at all, but curled up on the couch at home, eating chips and playing a video game.

Leaves closer by shook. Jude gasped and took a step back on the rotting log, trying to rebalance himself. Instead, he stepped into mid-air. He fumbled, tried to catch the closest branch. His hands gripped nothing but open air.

Jude fell with a crash to the ground below. He yelped and jumped up and then started to run. Branches scratched at his cheeks and roots and low-lying branches tried to trip him. He fell once, jerked back up, and started running again.

Mom. Dad. Tears pushed against the backs of Jude's eyes. Why had he left? He was going to die out here.

He shoved himself through a densely-packed group of trees and cried out as a branch whipped back across his cheek. He could feel a trickle of blood but didn't bother to wipe it away. Instead, he kept running. Waiting for whatever was behind him to launch itself at his back.

Chapter 12

Rick Langlois

Blue arcs of hot pain erupted in Rick's leg when he tried to shift his position in bed. He groaned and lay back, immobilized. There were blankets on him again, suffocating and hot. He tried to push them away but his arms were weak and shaky. He could smell something strange. It didn't belong in their bedroom. What was it? A musky, wild smell: almost like deer but different. Rick clenched his teeth and tried to shift again. He needed to get up. Figure out what was wrong with his leg. Why did it burn like that?

He was exhausted though and couldn't rouse himself. He heard a noise. Was it in their bedroom or outdoors? No, must be outside. It sounded like…coyotes.

Rick frowned. He should double-check to make sure Beanie was in for the night. No, that's right, Beanie was dead. Had been for a couple of years. Rick shivered suddenly. The sound of the coyotes was getting closer. They must be right outside the window. He should get up, chase them off. They were too close to the house. Marion wouldn't like it. Was she here? He couldn't feel her laying next to him.

Rick tried to open his eyes but they felt weighted shut. There was a bitter taste in his mouth and he was thirsty. It felt like he'd had a few—no a dozen—too many last night. But had he? His brain was like oatmeal, thick, and sludgy.

Where was Marion? Was Jude up already? Why was it so hot in here?

The eerie sound of the coyotes yipping drew closer.

Chapter 13

Marion Langlois

When Marion had first gotten her driver's license she'd been followed in a dark parking lot. It had been Christmas and she'd left the country club, elated that she could now just make an appearance, speak politely to Mother and Dad's friends and clients and then leave. She'd been struggling with an errant heel, she remembered, when she'd noticed that someone was following her. They moved between the cars just paces behind her. She'd listened, not sure if she should yell, turn to face them or ignore them, and hope they went away.

She remembered the sensation the most: the feeling of being hunted, being prey. She felt that same deep-seated fear now. It clawed up her chest and tightened her lungs as she looked at the pack of coyotes that drew closer to Rick.

Marion was too far to hit one of them with stones from here. Wasn't she? Still, if she could get them close enough to scare the pack away, it would give her time to climb back down and figure out something to keep them away more permanently.

They were getting closer, but slowly. They seemed skittish. Marion had always thought they were nocturnal animals, only coming out to hunt at night. But either the smell of fresh blood or their hunger must have driven them toward Rick.

She had to be fast. She scrabbled around the top of the cavern, picking up rocks of any size that she could throw. She wasn't sure how far away they were—she'd never been good at distances—but it seemed like they were at least eight stories below her.

She grunted as she launched the first stone over the side of the mountain. It fell too close to the side, bounced off rocks on its way down. It did, however, create a noise. The rock cracked against others and three of the coyotes glanced back, then danced around nervously in place. Marion grabbed two more stones and lobbed them at the pack one after the other. The first one got within a yard and the dog at the rear of the pack, mostly hidden by the leaves, jumped and turned, snarling. The second stone Marion had thrown did even better. It pinged one of the coyotes in the back leg. It yelped and jumped, causing the others to look around anxiously.

Still, they weren't turning back. They moved more slowly now, looking around them, but drawing closer to Rick. Damn. Marion wasn't sure how much further she could lob a rock. If only she had a flare gun or a bow and arrow. The thought of shooting one nearly made her laugh. A week ago she'd have told anyone who suggested it that it would never happen in this lifetime. Now, she desperately wished she had some of the survival skills that Rick had learned as a kid.

Biting her lip, Marion searched the ground and found a smooth, flat stone. Maybe if she threw it like a frisbee, as though she were trying to skip rocks at the beach...

She took her time. Then she used an underhand throw and aimed directly for the lead coyote's head. The stone sailed through the air, perfectly descending, and hit the first dog—the biggest one—just under its ear. Its head snapped back and it yelped, then turned, snarling at the two coyotes closest to it. They backed up, yipping and prancing, their ears back and their eyes downcast.

One of them keened and then two more joined in. There were six all together, Marion counted. Six of them and one of her. But they were leaving. Her breathing was hard as she watched first the biggest one—the alpha—turn and jog back into the woods the way it had come. The others soon followed.

Marion sagged against the side of the cavern. She wanted to give a victory shout but was too shaken. Instead, she turned and lowered herself over the edge of the cavern's top, using branches, the occasional sapling, and large stones to ease her way back down to the ground. Going up, it turned out, was easier than down. Marion's hands were slippery with sweat and more than once she started to fall, grabbed onto a root or branch of anything else sturdy, and stopped herself. She was nearly to the bottom—she could see the ground just five or so feet away—when the branch she was holding onto broke in her hands.

Screaming, Marion tried to grab onto something, anything else, that would stop her fall. But her hands felt only open air. She saw the rocks above her and then the sky and then she fell with a hard grunt on the ground. She'd landed on her back and couldn't breathe. She stared up at the leaves twirling in the breeze and tried not to panic.

Finally, her lungs opened and she gulped in air. Every one caused a sharp pain in her left side. Marion groaned and slowly pushed herself up into a sitting position. *I'm okay, I'm okay, I'm okay.* She repeated the words like a mantra in her head as she picked her way down the rest of the rocks.

If she was going to keep the coyotes away, she'd need to build a fire. A nice, big one. And burn everything that was scented with blood before it drew other predators.

Rick lay in the same position as when she'd left. She eased herself down next to him, sweat trickling along the center of her back.

"How are you doing, honey?" Marion asked, smoothing Rick's sweat-soaked hair back from his forehead. He was still so pale. "Please, hang in there. I'm going to get you out of here, I promise." Marion pressed a kiss onto her fingers and pressed that to Rick's cheek. She got him to swallow three more sips of water before he moaned and turned his head away. It might help to give him more of the pain medicine, but there weren't many left and she wanted to space them out as much as possible.

Marion left Rick under the blanket and started to collect wood for the fire. Small branches could be used for kindling and larger pieces from downed logs would be best for keeping the fire going. She'd never actually made a fire before. At home they had a gas fireplace and creating fire there was as easy as flipping a switch. But she'd seen Rick do it often in the summer. They had a beautiful fire area just outside of her flower garden. Rick had taught Jude and he, in turn, had tried to teach Marion.

She'd never really grasped it, had just nodded along to show her support of his skills. Still, how hard could it be?

***

Making a fire, it turned out, was next to impossible. Marion

83

had collected lots of wood and even some grass to get the fire started. She remembered something about building a teepee structure with the materials, so she'd laid out the big chunks as the base and made a tent with small kindling, sprinkling the grasses and dried leaves on top. But nothing was working out.

It would be easier with the waterproof matches that had been in the Emergency Kit, but Jude had taken that with him. She'd sat with a small magnifying glass that she'd found on Rick's Swiss army knife for more than an hour. She'd pointed the light directly at the grasses, waiting and waiting for them to erupt in flames.

Nothing happened.

She'd taken a break: had a half of an orange and a few sips of water and gotten some orange juice into Rick along with one of the crushed ibuprofen tablets. She'd found a flint on the jackknife too, but wasn't sure how to use it. What would you strike against it to make a fire? She tried a stick but that didn't work, then a small stone. Finally, after what felt like hours, Marion saw the tiniest flick of spark erupt from the flint. She cheered and waved a tired arm over her head in victory.

Ten sparks later and the grass finally caught. Instead of burning up the kindling though, it just burned up the grass. Then the fire went out. Marion wanted to cry again but wouldn't let herself.

This was ridiculous. How did pioneer women do it? They must have made fires every day out on the trail. What was she missing?

Matches, she thought bitterly. A blowtorch. Lighter fluid.

But maybe there was something else...

Marion studied the setup of the logs and kindling. It was

backward, she realized in chagrin. She'd reversed the order of the materials. The bigger things were supposed to be on top, not the bottom. Marion groaned and pulled everything out of the makeshift campfire ring and started over. This time, she layered the little twigs and small sticks over each other on the ground, leaving some room between for the air to get through. Fire needed air, that much she did know. After that, she propped up the larger branches around the small ones, making a little tent over them. Lastly, she tucked fresh, dried grass and leaves underneath the teepee structure. She held her breath and tried to light it again. She was getting better with the flint and after only three strikes, had a spark big enough to catch the grass on fire. She blew on it gently and smelled the wonderful, sweet smell of smoke.

Yes, yes, yes. Keep going, she willed the flames. They licked eagerly at the grass and Marion grinned. But the smile slipped from her face when again, the flames went out without igniting the kindling.

No! Why was that happening? Why wasn't it catching?

Marion leaned back to stretch out the kinks in her neck. As she did, she saw the note Jude had left, still attached to the little pad of paper. Maybe that would work?

Tearing the pages free carefully, Marion started with three. She made these into tiny, crumpled balls the same way Rick did with the newspaper he used to make fires at home. Then she tucked those into the kindling. Scrounging around the site, Marion found more dried grass and leaves and used these too, careful not to put so much in that there wasn't room for the fire to breathe.

She struck the flint again and again. Her arm ached and her fingers were covered in dirt and grime and slipped more than once off the stone she held in her hands. There! On the seventh strike the largest spark she'd created so far flared, igniting some of the grass and the first little ball of paper. Marion held her breath. The sun was dipping low into the trees which meant that nightfall wasn't too far away. She hadn't seen or heard the coyotes since early this afternoon but didn't want to without some measure of protection between them and her and Rick.

The flames licked hungrily at the kindling, and some of the small branches turned orange as they began to burn. She was too tired to cheer again but did feel a smile crease her face.

She had made a fire. Marion couldn't remember when she'd ever felt as proud as she did at that moment.

Chapter 14

Rick Langlois

Rick could smell smoke. Where was it coming from? He saw something from the corner of his eye, but when he tried to turn his head in that direction whatever it was skittered out of sight again. He could tell it was dark though, black even, and large.

He was so cold. His teeth chattered together and he felt as though he was lying in a snowbank. But that would be softer. The bed here was really bad: lumpy and uneven. Something sharp jabbed into his left side but when he tried to roll over it felt like someone stuck a hot poker into his other leg. The pain took his breath away.

The smell of smoke was stronger. He should tell the others… his family. What were their names again? Mary. Joe. No, that wasn't right. For no reason, Rick felt like giggling. He remembered how his mother always had a Virginia Slim burning in the ashtray. They'd sit at the yellow laminate table in the kitchen, his mother still dressed in her waitress uniform. And even though her face had been tired and there were lines there that made Rick feel sad, she'd always chatted with him about school and teased him about the pretty girls in his class.

He remembered suddenly her ankles, how fat and puffy they would be when she'd get home. She'd put them up on one of the other chairs at the table with a groan. His father was on the road most weeks. He wondered suddenly if his mother had missed Dad.

Rick heard a groan now. Was it Mom? No, that was stupid. She'd been gone for years. He felt something smooth and cool against his forehead though, and then a voice—Marion, that was it—asking if he was okay. If he could take a little drink for her.

He tried. The water was hot and tasted bitter but he tried to swallow it. She wiped his mouth afterward and he tried to tell her thank you, tried to open his eyes but both were too hard. Instead, he felt the strange, syrupy blackness stealing over him again.

Wait, he wanted to say. I have to talk to you. But the other part of him welcomed the darkness. There was no pain there and things weren't so hard to remember or put together.

Chapter 15

Jude Langlois

He wasn't sure how long he'd been running, but when Jude finally stopped, his legs were shaking like Jell-O. His lungs pinched and burned and a side stitch knifed into his side. He climbed up the low-hanging branches of a nearby tree, nearly falling when his sweaty palms slipped from the wood. But he tightened his grasp and kept going until he was at least eight or ten feet off the ground.

Panting, he leaned against the tree, keeping his legs wrapped around the branch he was sitting on. He'd never been so scared in his entire life. And now he had to use the bathroom. He swatted tiredly at some mosquitoes by his head and ignored the feeling. Instead, he thought about what to do next.

It was after noon, but he wasn't sure how long after. Jude held up his fingers against the sky. About two fingers fit between where the sun would be overhead at noon—directly above him—and where it was now. So, maybe it was around two or three.

He waited for his breathing to return to normal and wondered what it was that had been chasing him. Then tried hard not to think about it. He ate a granola bar after downing half of his water bottle. Forget saving the water and food. He was thirsty and hungry now. Jude wiped the sweat off his forehead and face with the back of an arm and waited for his heartbeat to return to normal. His cheek stung where the branch had whipped across it. His legs felt bruised though he didn't bother inspecting them.

He needed to get back on track. Get back to the campground before nightfall. He shivered. Just the thought of staying out here, in the woods all alone made a new batch of sweat break out and a sick feeling filled his belly. He couldn't do it. He couldn't stay out here alone in the woods. Or maybe, the thought made him even more scared, not alone at all.

Extracting the compass from his pocket, Jude held it flat and watched the red arrow. It moved a little between two points before coming to a rest. But it wasn't pointing south anymore. Instead, the arrow lined up right between "s" and "e". That wasn't good. That meant that Jude had run off course. He'd need to correct it, but how? He could retrace his steps, at least the best he could remember from where he'd been.

Jude snorted.

No way.

He wasn't going back to wherever that thing was. It could be still waiting for him out there, waiting for him to walk by so it could pounce.

But what about here? Jude looked around from his perch. Something could be hiding here in the undergrowth and he'd never know it. Or what if whatever it was could climb trees? Goosebumps popped out on his arms and legs and he shivered, despite the heat. He had to do something, though. He couldn't just sit here. He sucked his bottom lip in between his teeth and thought about it.

Finally, he decided: he'd climb down and then just start walking south again from here. Hopefully, whatever it was that had been in the woods was long gone. Jude was sure it was. If it had been following him, he'd have seen signs of it by now. He looked around him again carefully, but there were no swaying branches or shaking leaves that meant something was moving around in the undergrowth.

I'm safe. I'm safe. There's nothing here.

Jude's arms and legs ached as he lowered himself branch by branch out of the tree. His shorts snagged on a dead limb and the shorts tore as he jerked his leg. When he was back down on the ground he celebrated by eating an orange. He peeled it with still-shaking hands and took a big bite. Then he flipped open the compass again. After lining up the arrow up with the "s" he started walking. Jude walked and walked and walked. The only thing that he stopped for was to check the compass.

One thing Jude hadn't thought about was that adventures could be so boring. There wasn't anyone to talk to, mosquitoes whined in his ears and bit him all over and he was really, really tired. Being a hero sort of sucked, Jude thought glumly, as he hauled himself over yet another downed tree. He thought about his parents as he checked the compass again.

What were they doing? Was Dad getting better? Jude felt a hard ball of fear in his chest, like someone with big hands was squeezing him there when he thought about the cavern and the giant bat that had hurt his father. If Jude had had his rifle with him—

A sound came from ahead of him. Jude stopped but the thing—whatever it was—stopped too. Panicky fear swept over him again. Whatever had been following him in the forest earlier had found him. It must be stalking him. People said that mountain lions stalked their victims so silently that you didn't know there was even a wild animal in the area... until it was too late.

Jude swallowed hard and tried to listen but it was hard to do in the forest. There was too much noise: birds calling and cawing, tree branches squeaking and the sound of the leaves and pine needles whispering when the wind pushed them together.

He couldn't hear anything. Maybe it had been his imagination. Jude wished he had taken time to make a weapon before leaving that morning. He remembered one time his cousin Bill had shown him all these primitive weapons he'd made on a Boy Scout trip with his dad. There had been spears and stakes made from tree branches and even throwing stars made from smaller branches and tied together with grass or something. Jude remembered too, feeling a pang of jealousy. Dad had been excited when Jude first joined Cub Scouts. But then he'd gotten too busy with the shop to take him to most of the meetings. Not that Jude had made a big deal out of it.

There was that sound again.

Jude stopped dead in his tracks. He listened harder. It sounded almost like—was it water? This time it didn't fade away like it had before. He looked at his compass. His path had drifted slightly to the southwest but it seemed like that's where the water was. It could be a brook. Or the lake.

The lake! If Jude could get there, he'd be saved. He knew he could find his way back to the campground from there. It would be easy. He hesitated: should he follow the water sounds or the compass? Water. Anyway, he could refill his water bottle. And even if it was just a brook, it might be the same one that led to the lake like the one him and Dad had found yesterday. The water sounds were getting really loud now. Maybe he'd put his feet in for a little while and wash his face.

Jude hiked on, his legs aching and his stomach already growling again. It would feel good to get some more water. He probably wouldn't need it—he was nearly back at camp he was sure—but it was a good idea to have extra with him. Anyway, that's what they'd always said in Cub Scouts: it was one of the three essentials: water, food, shelter. But he wasn't going to need the last one. There was no way he'd be out here tonight. He pictured his warm sleeping bag—or better yet, his bed—and smiled.

A squirrel crashed through some undergrowth to his right. Jude glanced over, distracted. And when his foot came down it hit nothing but air. Jude gasped, then cried out. What had before been solid earth had turned into a drop. Jude yelled and tried to grab onto roots, branches, anything that would save him.

Instead, he fell freely through the air. Seconds later, he hit the cold, rushing water below and went under.

I'm drowning, a panicked little voice in his head screamed. His lungs burned but when he got his head above the water, a big splash of it churned into his face and he choked on it. He kicked hard with his legs and tried to get up to the surface again. Something hit his head and fireworks exploded across his skull. The water churned around him, brown and gray. Jude couldn't tell which way was up.

He was going to die out here. He was drowning.

The water shoved him hard and his arm crashed into something solid. He grabbed onto it. It was rough and hard under his hands. A log that was also being shoved by the powerful current. Jude's head broke through the surface of the water and he took in two huge gasps before he went under again. This time though, he knew which was up. He kicked hard and broke through the surface of the water again. He gasped and choked and held onto the branch for dear life. It bobbed and swayed with the current.

Once it nearly knocked him off when it started turning in a circle but Jude hung on. He gripped the log so tightly his arms and fingers tingled.

He looked around him, tried to get his bearings. It was a river or a big brook. Up ahead Jude heard a sound that stopped his heart.

Rushing, powerful water.

A waterfall.

No, no, no.

Jude kicked twice as hard, even though his legs felt like spaghetti noodles. He was closer to the shore to his left, so he aimed his body in that direction the best he could and kicked. The log was getting in his way, making his kicking less effective and rolling and twisting in the current but Jude didn't want to let go. Finally, though, he had to. The log was pulling him downstream, toward the waterfall. Jude took a huge breath and let go, then swam the rest of the way to the side of the river. His strokes were jerky and weak and he got water up his nose, then in his throat. He coughed and swam until he managed to grab some of the exposed tree roots along the bank. The water continued to pull at him, trying to yank him downstream, but Jude held on.

"Help!" he yelled, even though he knew no one could hear him.

He gripped the roots and slowly started to pull himself up

the bank. It was a sharp drop, not like at a beach, and Jude's pack pulled him in the other direction. He should get it off but he didn't have his arms free and didn't dare let go of the roots.

Finally, finally, he managed to clamber onto the muddy riverbank. The mud was oozy and smelled like the bathroom at school after Henry Hughes used it. Jude gagged through his panting. He was so glad to be on land again though that he almost kissed the dirty ground.

He rolled over onto his back and closed his eyes. He focused on breathing, big gulps of air in and out, in and out.

He'd almost died. Jude thought of his parents and friends at school. Tears started rolling down his face and he lay there for a few long minutes, breathing and gasping and spitting out river water. Snot and tears mixed on his face.

After he'd calmed down a little, Jude rolled over onto his stomach and pushed himself up. His clothes and hair dripped, dirty water gushing every time he moved. He mopped his face with the sleeve of his wet shirt. It came away pink. Jude explored his forehead, wincing when his fingers felt a cut about three inches long. He held his arm there for a few seconds, then slowly stood up. His legs shook so hard he nearly fell back over. He balanced himself on a tree, held his arm up to his forehead again.

Now what?

The sun had dipped lower in the sky. What time was it now? Four o'clock. Maybe later. Jude shivered hard. His pack was still on his back. One of the straps was twisted though and dug uncomfortably into his arm. Before he pulled it off, he checked his pocket, looking for the compass.

A sick, cold feeling spread through his belly.

It was gone.

Chapter 16

Marion Langlois

The fire was blazing and Marion had curled on her side and watched it. Rick was at her back and every few minutes he shifted and moaned. She'd given him another dose of pain medicine and gotten the other half of the orange—or at least its juice—into him. But it didn't seem to be doing much good.

Marion bit her lip and let out a frustrated breath. What else could she do? And how long did he have before the infection spread to the point of no return? She needed antibiotics, but there was no chance of finding those out here.

Evening was falling and the sounds in the forest around them changed. From birdsong to crickets and other, softer night noises she didn't recognize. The air was filled with the smell of woodsmoke and pine and, despite the dire situation they were in, Marion couldn't help but smile as she looked overhead. Early evening stars had sprouted in the sky and the blue was a beautiful indigo shade.

Sitting up caused her head to start pounding again. It felt like there was a drum corps up there, keeping time against the edges of her skull. What was she going to do? The fire might keep the coyotes away. Maybe. If they were lucky. But she'd feel much better if she had a weapon of some sort. And there was one…it was just deep inside the cavern.

Marion pressed her lips together, thinking. Was it worth it? Worth retracing her steps and getting the knife? If she had it, she thought she could make a spear. All she'd need to do was whittle away the end of the branch. The thought of a spear in her hand and bowie knife strapped to her leg felt good.

She didn't want to do this. The last thing in the world she wanted was to go back into that cavern. She sighed and stood up. But getting the knife was important to their survival.

Who knew how long they'd be stuck out here? Their camping reservation had been for three nights. This would make night two, which meant that there was at least another two days and one night before anyone even realized they were missing. Rick had taken Monday off at the garage so no one would expect him before Tuesday. Jude was on summer break and Marion had so little contact with friends or her parents that it would be days, maybe even weeks before anyone in her circle realized something was amiss. By then she'd be dead.

She shook her head. She wasn't going to die out here and neither was Rick or Jude if she could help it. She'd go back to the cave and get the knife. Right now it was all about options. The more the better. And having the knife opened up options that she didn't have otherwise.

Pushing away thoughts about getting lost in the cavern, or the coyotes coming back and mauling Rick while she was gone, Marion stood. She swayed a little, held onto the closest tree until the dizziness passed. If only Jude hadn't—

But he had, Marion reminded herself, so she needed to do what she could on her own. Doing outdoor things was something that Marion wasn't comfortable with. Heading up a bake sale at school? No problem. Bringing her artwork to the local gallery and hanging a display? She was confident doing that without issue. Hosting a party in her garden for her gardening club friends? Absolutely. But protecting herself and her husband from wild animals? Trying to keep someone alive who was burning up with fever from an infection? Surviving in the wilderness for who-knew-how-long?

Marion shivered but then straightened her back. She might be Rick's only hope. The thought made her more afraid and a little angry all at the same time. That was good, she thought as she gathered a few supplies: a flashlight and a pointed stick she'd found near Rick. The anger felt good. It could fuel her. The pointed stick wasn't a real weapon but might work in a pinch. She wrapped her hands up like a boxer's, winding more strips of canvas over her palms with her fingers sticking out. The part of the tunnel she was dreading most was the narrow spot where she'd have to crawl. She pushed away images of the huge bat with its snarling gray face and the hundreds of others circling above. They had to be gone by now, surely.

Marion fed more logs onto the fire, making sure there were enough to keep it going but not enough to smother it. She waited for them to catch and smoothed a hand over Rick's forehead. He quieted a little, seemed less agitated. It brought tears to her eyes.

She kissed his forehead, then put her own against his. Willing him to hear her thoughts, feel the love she was sending him. "I'll be back soon," Marion said and kissed his forehead gently. It was burning hot. "I promise. And we'll get you help. Please don't give up on me."

Marion smoothed her hand once more over his forehead

and tucked the mylar blanket more tightly around him. He looked so much younger. So vulnerable. When was the last time they'd been vulnerable with each other? Marion and Rick had been having problems for a long time. And it wasn't all about the garage, either. It was everything: money, in-laws, power, raising Jude.

But Rick was a good man. He loved their son, loved her, even if they hadn't done a good job of being true partners for a long time. One of the things she'd loved most about Rick when they'd met was that he was willing to go his own way, to not follow conventional wisdom. That and the way that he had been enthralled with her.

She sighed, surveyed the area. There were a lot of branches on the ground, maybe blown down from a thunderstorm at some point. She remembered suddenly Rick telling Jude that pine pitch will act as a fire propellant. Not like gasoline, of course, but maybe it would keep the flames burning hot and bright. Marion found two pine branches thick with the sticky pine sap. She pushed those ends into the fire. At first, they just smoldered. Finally, flames broke out on the ends of each. Marion stuck them into the earth along the back side of where Rick was laying. He was unprotected there by the fire. Hopefully, if the coyotes came back, they'd be leery of the makeshift torches.

Marion looked around the camp again. She ignored the sick feeling in her stomach and ran through the layout of the cavern again in her mind. Because she'd been unconscious when she'd arrived, she'd have to remember and retrace her steps from their exit. She knew that first, she'd need to follow a straight path, then the tunnel would narrow. After that there was a turn—but had it been to the left or the right—Marion couldn't remember. When she got there, instinct would take over. She hoped anyway.

The sun had dropped a bit lower in the sky by the time she'd climbed back up to the cavern's entrance. She took one last glance around the forest before flicking on the flashlight and entering the tunnel. It smelled earthy and damp, like the garden when it was first turned over in the spring. Marion kept her head down and her eyes on the floor in front of her. All she needed was to trip and break an ankle. She walked on and on, her breathing and an erratic drip of water somewhere further back the only sounds.

The air in the cave became cooler the further in she walked. The tunnel narrowed. Marion felt relief. She remembered this part. After it, there would be a split—two or three ways that intersected, like lanes of traffic on the interstate. She eased through the tunnel, careful not to let her injured shoulders and back touch the low cave ceiling or damp walls.

There, ahead a "Y" formed in the darkened tunnel. But which way had they come, from the right or left? Marion bit her lip and squinted. Neither looked familiar. She'd been preoccupied with Rick, not focusing on her surroundings. So much for her recognizing it when she got there, Marion thought bitterly. She looked carefully at each tunnel again.

What should she do? If she chose wrong she could get lost. Besides, she didn't want to leave Rick alone too long. But then an image of the knife came to her—the long, reassuring blade. If only she'd grabbed it after she'd stabbed the bat. If only she'd...but that wasn't going to help her now.

Left, she thought. We came from that way. And if she was wrong and it was the other one, she'd retrace her steps. Walking quickly down the tunnel, she shone the flashlight around her every few steps. She wondered if something was watching her. She could sense another presence in the cave, something dark and animalistic.

But no, she was just on high alert. The giant bat was dead. And the other bats, for whatever reason, had flown off afterward. Perhaps they'd moved on to another room, or maybe there was a back entrance that she didn't know about. They could be flying low around the lake at this minute, just like they had been the night before.

Marion stumbled on a small, loose stone and caught herself on a boulder before falling. *Be careful. If something happens to you...*

She slowed her pace, looked more closely before moving her bandaged feet over the rock-littered floor of the tunnel. Surely, she should be at the cavern by now? She tried to remember how long it had taken when they'd left. She remembered a narrow opening, and that it was high up. She shone her flashlight around and above her but didn't see anything.

It was hard to remember because she and Jude had been supporting Rick who could barely stumble. Marion hadn't exactly been paying attention to their path, just letting Jude lead the way. Besides, in desperate situations like that time seemed to move more slowly.

But was she going in the wrong direction? Every step could be taking her further away from the knife. She paused a second, rested against the wall.

Did anything look familiar? She swung the flashlight in front of her and then behind. Not really. Everything looked the same in either direction: a long, narrow space filled with tons of rocks of all different sizes.

Marion glanced at her watch. She'd continue in this

direction for another five minutes. If she hadn't found the cavern by then, she'd retrace her steps and head the other way. Marion started walking again. Soon, she felt something against her cheeks. Strange, it felt like a breeze. Cool air wafted over her and she breathed deeply. It smelled of the outdoors, sweet and warm, and welcome. Only…this meant that Marion had gone the wrong way. Dread pressed against her ribs and burned in the back of her throat.

Sure enough, seconds later her flashlight beam hit a large boulder. Above it was a direct opening to the forest. She could see bits of the pine tree and a large swath of sky. She'd chosen wrong, had ended up on the far end of the tunnel. She was standing in the opposite direction of Rick now. The thought made her feel like screaming.

What was that? A noise behind her like a strong wind came through the tunnel. Marion closed her eyes and shook her head. She was tired, too tired to deal with anything else.Part of her felt angry too, that she'd been reduced to this. Hiding and sniveling in the shadows of this stupid tunnel in the middle of nowhere.

But she ducked anyway and flicked off her light. The sound of bat wings—hundreds, maybe thousands of them—filled the tunnel. Marion crouched behind a big stone and held in a scream. She pulled herself into a ball, arms over her head. Her shoulders, raw beneath Rick's T-shirt pressed painfully into the unforgiving stone behind her, but Marion didn't care. She closed her eyes and prayed. And waited for tiny, jagged teeth to tear into her.

The sound went on forever, like an ocean wave that refused to crest. Marion felt dizzy and realized she'd stopped breathing. She let the air out of her lungs and snuck a peek upward.

Hundreds of dark wings were illuminated against the pale evening sky. Bats poured from the tunnel in thick, black waves. The leftover ammonia scent of guano hung in the air for a long time after they'd gone. Marion just sat still, waiting and waiting for another colony to fly through. But no more flew through the air.

Finally, she rose to a standing position. Was it over? Were they gone? She flicked on her light and shone it around. A single, errant bat flew by. It flew jerkily out of the tunnel and into the night. Marion stood for a few seconds and tried to make her limbs stop shaking. Then she retraced her steps. This time at the split, she chose the tunnel to the right. Minutes later, she saw what she'd been looking for earlier: a hole high up in the cave wall. She remembered this now, the way that the big boulder underneath it acted like a slide when they'd lowered Rick through.

"The packs were there," she said out loud, surprised by the sound of her voice. Somehow it made her feel better. Less alone.

"They were there, and we climbed down and grabbed them."

She hauled herself upward, over the smaller rocks and stones, and finally over the much larger one. She took her time squeezing through the narrow opening, tried not to think of what might be waiting for her on the other side.

She emerged from the opening, back into the cavern. The smell hit her first, followed by the colder air. Swallowing hard, Marion looked around her. The room was like a giant amphitheater. She stared at the place where she'd been thrown. It was still streaked with black goo and most likely some of her blood. Suddenly, Marion started shaking. She shuddered hard enough that the flashlight threatened to come out of her hand. Unnerved at the thought of losing it, she reached over and held it tightly with both hands.

Get in and get out, that's what she needed to do, she thought. Not dredge up things from the night before. Not remember the panic she'd felt when she'd come to, or the horror of seeing the giant bat with its claws stabbed into Rick. Not feel the debilitating fear when she'd seen Jude in this horrible place, with his frightened eyes and too-pale skin. *Keep it together* a little voice whispered. *Get the knife and get out of here.*

She surveyed the room carefully. The big bat—she'd killed it there, hadn't she? She glanced around and frowned. She was sure that was the place. She edged a little closer. Could her mind be playing tricks on her? But no, as she drew nearer she saw some dark stains where its blood hand run over the stones. But there was no bat. Other than the pungent smell, there was no sign of bats, giant or otherwise, in the cavern.

Marion made her way down the steep wall, taking time to find her foot and handholds fully before every descent. She clenched the flashlight between her teeth and gagged at the taste of dirt and who knew what else that coated it. When she got to the place where the floor of the cave could be felt under her feet, she let go of the stones on the wall and hung onto the flashlight again.

That was definitely the spot where Rick and the bat had been. But where was the knife? Marion flicked the light this way and that. There was no glint of a sharp blade. But it had to be here. There was no way it couldn't be, not now when she'd come all this way.

Marion moved closer to inspect the area more fully. There! Stuck between two rocks was the handle of the black knife. She only noticed it because the brand name was written in small, white letters that practically glowed in the dark space. Marion grabbed at the handle and with a little pulling, managed to free it from the stones. Relief poured over her like hot shower water. She held the knife in one hand the flashlight in the other. Now all she had to do was climb back up out of the cavern and retrace her steps to the front entrance. It would be—

A sound filled the cavern. Slow at first, like the rough whisper of dry leaves flying across a paved road. Then louder. And even louder. And then another noise filled the giant room: the unmistakable hiss she'd heard here before.

Marion looked wildly around her. Where was it? Where in the—her thought ended in a moan of fear. Above her, about ten feet to her right was a familiar shape. No. Not just one. Three familiar shapes. They sat like gargoyles perched high up on a stone slab. Three big bats. Each one with a pushed in gray face. The one closest to her had its teeth bared. The hissing sound came from between its jagged teeth that were covered in drool. It ran from its large, half-open mouth.

Marion held in a scream. She turned and started to climb. Clawing her way over stones and boulders, she didn't bother to make sure she had good stability. Instead, she launched herself onto the next one and the next. She nearly lost the flashlight and only held onto it and the knife because they felt welded to her palms. She held on so tightly that she imagined they were leaving marks. Every so often the knife clinked on a stone or rock. Marion panted and listened behind her for the hissing.

It got louder. Another bat had joined in. Marion chanced a look over her shoulder and screamed.

Two of the three bats swooped toward her. Marion dove

for a big boulder and let the weight of her body carry her over it. She plunged headfirst into a narrow crevasse. Above her, was the heavy flap of wings and then the hissing became even louder. Marion pulled her legs into the space and gasped as one of the bats plunged its head deep into the opening between the rocks. She tried to swing at it with the blade but her hand was underneath her. She'd thrown her hands out instinctively and didn't know where the knife had gone.

Frantically, she felt around the rocks and stones beneath her. Her hand hit something metal and she grabbed it and jerked her hand upward. It was the flashlight. She flicked it on and shone it directly into the nearest bat's face.

It squealed and turned its ugly face away. Marion remembered going on a field trip to a farm once in grade school. The sound the bat made reminded her of a mother pig. An angry one who didn't appreciate third graders trying to pet her babies.

Relief ran into every capillary in Marion's body. She shone the flashlight all around her. It created a little bubble, she thought, a bubble of light that would protect her. Half paying attention, she fumbled around the rocks underneath her for the knife. Her hand closed over the hilt and she jerked it upward.

When the second bat's face appeared over the opening, Marion was ready. Her arm shot upward toward its face. But the creature veered out of the way and the blade cut only into the open air. Another hiss, a loud squeal, and then the second bat's head reappeared. It was blind, Marion realized as she took another wild swing. Its eyes were cloudy white and unlike the first bat, it wasn't at all afraid of the flashlight's beam.

The bat was close, so close that Marion smelled its rotten-meat scented breath and heard its teeth grinding against each other. She waited this time, anticipating the bat's move. It reared its head back and then dove down toward her. Marion tightened her grip on the knife's handle and swung it upward as hard as she could. It wasn't a good hit because the narrow space between the stones prevented her from using the force she needed. But the blade cut across the bat's face and it drew back in pain, screaming. Marion dropped her head between her arms and pressed her forearms over her ears. The bat continued to screech as it pulled itself free from the tight enclosure. Marion remained prone on the ground and stayed there until she heard the flapping sound and hissing fade away.

Chapter 17

Rick Langlois

What had woken him? Rick's eyelids fluttered, strained to stay open. Focus, dammit! He squinted, managed to keep them open long enough to see around him. Woods. Night. Orange glow of flames. Fire-like pain ripped down his leg as he turned over. He cemented his jaws together and forced himself to an elbow. Then he blinked in a slow, exaggerated motion until finally, they focused.

The woods around him were dark. The silhouettes of trees high above like black fingers stabbing at the dark-blue sky. Everything was blurry at first. He blinked a few more times which helped. He was laying on some clothes, more were scattered around in front of him. There was a fire that was burning down. The flames shimmered and the smell of smoke was heavy in the air. From the number of coals, it must have been burning a while.

He surveyed the space in a long, slow circle—partly because he didn't want to miss anything, partly because his head was throbbing. He was half under a big pine tree, the boughs low enough to hide some of the stars. It hadn't prevented someone—Jude? Marion?—from making the fire. Behind him were makeshift torches that were nearly burned out.

Where were they? Where had everyone gone? Rick shivered even though sweat trickled through his scalp and down his back. He was overheated and pushed the space blanket off him. He needed to get his bearings. Figure out what was going on.

"Mar...Marion?" he called quietly and was surprised to hear how weak his voice was.

Think. He needed to figure this out.

What did he remember last? The cavern. Jude, almost falling. The smell, thick and choking had made his eyes water. And then...what? He pressed a hand to his temple, felt cloth there, and a painful spot. What had happened then? A light. They'd seen a light and then—Rick felt a horrible knot of nausea form in his belly and thought he might be sick.

And then all the bats...so many he couldn't have counted them if he'd tried. And the one giant one had grabbed him—he shut his eyes suddenly. Turned to the side of where he lay and retched but nothing came out. The pounding in his head was worse. Part of him wanted to lay back down.

He was so thirsty though. It felt like he'd been walking in a desert for days. Where was the water? He looked around him and saw a bottle near where his head had been moments before. Rick lifted it to his mouth. Or tried to. It sloshed and shook in his hand. He might as well be trying to lift a thirty-inch truck tire. He tried again this time using both hands. He put his lip under the rim and tipped it back. More water ran down his chin and chest than ended up in his mouth. What little he did manage to swallow though, tasted wonderful, plastic flavoring and all.

His hands trembled as he lowered the bottle back down. He wasn't sure if there was more water and didn't want to waste what little was left. He wiped the back of his hand over his mouth and tried to push himself a little more upright. He groaned as the fire restarted arcing down his leg. But there was another sound over that. Something…wild. An animal moving through the undergrowth? Rick listened over the thud of his heartbeat. Seconds later, there were more sounds, these louder than before. It sounded like…Like a herd of something moving. Maybe it was deer? But a second sound soon followed and Rick's heart jumped in his chest as he recognized it. A low growl came from the far side of the small clearing. Rick saw branches move and shake as many bodies slunk through the woods. He felt his stomach drop the same as it had at the summer fair when Jude had begged him to try the rollercoaster.

Coyotes.

How many? Even one was too many now. Rick wanted to close his eyes, sink back onto the earth, and rest. Instead, he kept his eyes open, scanned the trees and undergrowth for a sign of the predators.

There.

The tip of an ear poked out from the overgrowth near the clearing. A second later, a gray muzzle sniffed the air as the coyotes crept closer. Rick had to think. Had to do something. But what? He was weak and helpless. He didn't have his gun. A glance at his leg told him that his knife was also missing.

But there was the fire. He could build it up. Maybe get the torches burning again.

"Marion?" he called again softly. If she was nearby she could help him. "Marion?" his voice was pathetically weak. Rick

111

looked at the wood. Marion or Jude had broken some pieces and made a little pile. It lay between him and the fire. It might as well have been a mile away. Rick closed his eyes. Then heard a yip. He jerked himself forward on his good arm and nearly collapsed. Lightning shot up the side of his body and coursed through his leg. He felt something wet ooze.

Not bothering to take the time to inspect his leg, Rick pulled himself along the ground, crawling on his elbows. It was only a couple of feet away. Just a couple. He could do it. He was going to do it. He didn't have a choice.

A keening cry of one of the coyotes split the air. All the hair on Rick's body stood up simultaneously. He gasped then groaned. Misjudging the next forward movement, he smacked his good elbow hard into a rock embedded in the ground. Ignoring the pain, he continued crawling.

Finally, he was there and reached a hand out. The nearest piece of wood was dry but thick. Too thick for the fire. He'd have to use something smaller. He fumbled around, trying to keep one eye on the pack of coyotes and the other on what he was doing. His hand closed around a thinner piece. He grabbed it, threw it back toward the fire. He gasped at the pain in his leg and side but didn't stop. Instead, he grabbed two more pieces and threw them closer to the fire, too.

He kept moving forward, toward the fire. The flames were anemic, with more smoke than the actual fire. Would he be able to build it back up in time? Rick tried not to think of what would happen if he couldn't. The coyotes could smell blood. And they had to be hungry to come this close to a human. He glanced toward the tree line again and then wished he hadn't. They were closer. The branches and leaves told of their approach, though so far they'd hung back, remained in the underbrush.

"Hey!" Rick yelled or tried to. It came out like a strangled whisper. He grimaced and tried again. "Hey! Get out of here!"

He pushed the first and smallest dead branch onto the fire. It immediately started to smolder. Smoke thick and sweet-smelling choked Rick as he moved his face out of the cloud to breathe. He moved his head a few inches, then blew on the fire. It smoked some more. Then a few little flames ignited, licking the bottom of the branch. But when Rick stopped to draw another breath, the flames died.

One of the coyotes began to howl, a chilling series of notes that sent dread along with acid rushing up Rick's throat. He blew on the fire again and again. Dizzy, he squinted into the fire. Again, the flames would ignite and engulf the wood, only to return to smoldering once he stopped blowing. He could hear his heartbeat between yips and barks. Sweat coated his face and arms and his leg was dripping with blood under the pad over it. Rick wanted to yell in frustration but concentrated on blowing more air onto the sickly fire.

The coyotes drew closer. He could hear them panting now, between yips. They sounded like a cross between wolves and hyenas, their chilling cries overlapping. Then one dog—a large one—jogged out of the line of trees. It stood in the clearing, maybe seventy feet away. It looked at Rick and sniffed the air. It was large—solid and gray with muscular shoulders. Only the alpha would eat so well as to be that fleshed out. Rick swallowed and blew harder. The coyote threw its head back and let out a signature howl. Before the last notes had faded others joined in. The sound froze Rick's blood and made his throat close over. He couldn't breathe on the fire. He couldn't breathe at all. Maybe it wouldn't be so bad. He could just stop breathing and pass out. Would he remain unconscious when they started to eat him? Or wake up in time to feel their teeth slice through his skin?

A rush of flame shot up from the new branch. The smoke cleared as the fire licked hungrily at the fresh wood. The big coyote stopped mid-howl and pranced back on its feet. Two more dogs joined the first but they hung back, closer to the trees.

"Get outta here!" Rick yelled. This time his voice cooperated, maybe because of the surplus of adrenaline coursing through his system. The big coyote stepped forward, growled. Rick thought he might piss himself.

"Get out!" Rick yelled again. Then he dipped the tip of the second fresh piece of wood into the fire. He alternated looking at the coyotes and watching the branch slowly become engulfed in flames. When it was burning, he lifted it in the air. His arm shook wildly. The branch felt as heavy as a forty-pound barrel.

"Out!" Rick poked the air menacingly toward the coyotes. Again, the big one took a step back. The other two jogged back into the trees, though kept looking over their shoulders as they did so. The keening turned back into yips. Then a shadow moved through the woods. A pale gray-white coyote joined the first one. This one was smaller but its lips were drawn back, showing its fangs. It growled with its head lowered and Rick's stomach flipped.

The big one growled again, the sound deeper and more commanding. The smaller one—Rick guessed it was the alpha female—crept a couple of steps closer toward him. Her teeth were still bared, pale yellow in the firelight. Rick couldn't help but notice how large and sharp they were. He shook the branch again overhead, realizing how pathetic and useless the motion was. There was no way he could fend off a single coyote, let alone a pack, with the strength and meager defenses he had. But what other options did he have?

The smaller coyote drew closer. Her growl was low and menacing. Her ears were flattened against her head and she'd crouched even lower. Any minute, Rick expected her to launch herself at him, to feel her teeth tearing into him. It felt like time had come to a standstill. There were only him and the coyote. The fire and the wide vastness of the woods around them. He could taste the fear on his tongue, bitter and sharp. He smelled the musky odor of wild animals in the air.

He pulled his arm behind his head and with a grunt, threw the flaming branch toward the female. She yipped as it caught her on the side of the face, then fell onto one of her feet. She danced backward, made a series of cries, then snarled and lunged toward Rick.

The alpha male jumped forward, caught her in the shoulder, and nipped her back. She cried out again and then turned and ran back into the woods. The alpha followed without another glance at Rick. Branches and leaves shook as the pack loped away. But Rick didn't dare move an inch from the fire until he couldn't see the movements anymore.

Then he sank onto the ground and shook all over.

Chapter 18

Jude Langlois

Moron. *Idiot. Screwup.*

The little voice in Jude's head repeated these over and over as he turned, shivering on the bank of the river, and tried to figure out where he was. How could he have lost the compass? It was the one thing he needed to get out of the woods. He'd never find his way back to camp now. He sank to his knees, felt a mixture of anger and shame as warm wet trails ran down his cheeks. Putting his hands over his face, he blubbered like a baby for a full minute or two. It felt good and humiliating at the same time. He wished Mom was here to hug him and tell him that everything was going to be okay. And that Dad was standing right next to her, embarrassed enough by Jude's tears to look away, but not so much that he'd leave. Jude wished it so hard that he could almost feel his father's big, warm hand on his shoulder.

Finally spent, Jude wiped his face on his wet T-shirt. He needed to do something. He couldn't just sit here bawling until he died. He had to try to get back to camp, to save his parents. They needed him.

Jude remembered a chapter book that him and Dad had

started reading together over the winter. Dad had felt guilty that he wasn't home more—probably because Mom nagged him about it all the time—and so he'd told Jude that they'd better prepare for this summer's big camping trip. His father had found this old book from when he was a kid—*Hatchet*—about a boy who gets lost in the wilderness and has to survive. Jude had forgotten about it, mostly because they'd only read a few chapters before Dad started working late again.

But Jude thought about the boy in the book now. Brian, that had been his name. Jude knew that he wasn't as smart as Brian in the woods. But he was awesome at video games. And the one thing any good gamer knows is when to make a new strategy. This usually happened after Jude had lost a few lives. But the more he played, the faster he got at figuring out the situation and making new plans in seconds.

So, if this was a video game, what would he do next? He was lost. The compass was gone. His pack was soaked but he still had it. He wasn't seriously hurt.

What did he need?

A new plan.

First, he needed to get dry. Even though the afternoon air wasn't cold, he shivered hard from the soaking. Next, he needed to find a place to stay for the night. It would be dark before long and while Jude was freaked out at the thought of staying in the woods alone through the long, night, he knew it was probably going to happen. He couldn't wander around in the dark. He'd get even more lost. Maybe even eaten. Jude thought about that thing in the undergrowth and his stomach squeezed uncomfortably.

So, first fire. Then shelter.

He pulled the pack free and dug through it. He hoped he hadn't lost anything else in the river. The extra clothes were still there but soaked. There was a single orange left and two mashed granola bars. His paperback copy of *White Fang* was completely ruined as was the newest zombie book in the series he'd been reading. He tossed them aside into the brush, but then thought better of it. Maybe if he could start a fire, he could dry them out.

What about the matches? He clawed through the rest of his bag. Had they fallen out? He searched the entire bag, dumping everything out on the ground. No, there they were! Rolled between an extra shirt was the little canister of waterproof matches. Jude felt a happy glow in his chest. He'd make a fire. Dry things out and warm up. And then he'd build a shelter for the night.

***

It turned out that starting a fire wasn't as easy as he'd expected. Though the waterproof matches flared and kept a good, strong flame, the grass and leaves he'd found were too damp to catch fire. He'd tried, again and again, getting more and more frustrated and losing more and more matches. Finally, he'd had to move away from the river, up a little hill where the air was drier.

By the time the fire was glowing brightly, it was getting dark. Jude hadn't noticed how dark until the bright light of the fire started making shadows in the woods around him. Jude shivered hard, his teeth chattering as he held his hands up to the fire. He had to find somewhere to sleep safely. And he needed to dry himself off. But how?

He looked around him. The woods were dark and already spooky looking. The birds had almost stopped singing and now other sounds filled the air. He recognized crickets and the far-away twang of a tree frog, but that was it. Nothing rustled through the undergrowth at least and Jude was glad about that.

There wasn't time to make a shelter. And anyway—Jude checked the sky—it didn't look like it would rain. A bed would be nice though, instead of sleeping on the lumpy ground. He broke off some low-hanging pine branches, the clean, sweet smell filling the air. He laid those down next to the fire. On the other side, he laid out everything from his pack to dry out. Jude curled into a ball on the little nest of pine branches. It wasn't soft like his bed at home. Not even close. But it was better than nothing. The fire was warm at least. He'd almost stopped shivering.

Jude eyed the granola bars hungrily. He should wait until later. He didn't want to run out. But his stomach was so empty. He couldn't sleep like this. Finally, he reached across the fire and snagged one, ate the whole thing in four big bites. He drank some water and eyed the orange. But he'd better save it for breakfast.

What were his parents doing right now? Were they sitting around their own little fire, worried about him? Tears threatened to start again, but Jude shoved the image of his parents away. Instead, he thought about the morning, and what he'd do as soon as he woke up. But after a few seconds, Jude struggled to keep his eyes open. He should spread out the extra shirt and socks, they were all balled up on the other side of the fire. But his eyelids grew heavier and heavier. He slipped into a fitful sleep where the earth and sky had come together and he was drowning and flying all at the same time.

***

Something growled. Jude's eyes snapped open and he sat up, still damp, and tried to figure out where he was.

Woods.

Nighttime.

Alone.

Jude looked around the area frantically. He'd heard a growl...but had it been real or part of his strange dreams?

Footsteps. Coming this way. Through a hole in the undergrowth, Jude saw something large and furry coming toward him. He should jump up, yell, and wave his arms. But he was frozen to the spot. Ice ran through his arms and legs. They were so heavy they wouldn't move. Another growl, deep and low.

Then a bark.

Jude gasped.

Another bark.

Coyotes? Wolves? Jude's wide eyes scanned the area. At least his head still worked, even if his body didn't. Images flooded his brain: the giant bat, the whole bunch of other bats biting and clawing at his dad. The thing that had followed him in the woods. His heart slammed into his ribs and he was breathing so hard he thought he might pass out. The undergrowth nearby trembled, then shook. Then a short, furry head popped out just feet from where Jude was laying.

It was a dog. But unlike any dog, Jude had seen before. Its body was long but its legs were short and it had the biggest ears Jude had ever seen. They were so long and droopy that he was surprised the dog didn't trip on them.

The dog ran up to Jude, panting, and then whined. It wasn't close enough to touch him, but almost.

"Hey, boy," Jude said and put his shaking hand out toward the dog. "Where'd you come from?"

The dog cocked its head. Its tail was wagging so Jude scooted closer. The dog sniffed the air once, then took two steps toward Jude. Then it lunged at him, licked his face, and snuffled his neck. Jude laughed.

"What are you doing out here?" Jude asked again, but the dog just backed up a step and wagged its tail.

"Are you thirsty?"

The dog was panting and Jude guessed he'd been running awhile. There were little bits of white foam around its mouth. He remembered his grandfather's horse would get that after it had been running a long time. He pet the dog's head and it tried to lick him again. Jude moved his head and hugged the dog around the neck.

"I don't know your name but I'm really glad you found me." He sat back and grabbed his water bottle, uncapped it, and held it between his knees. Jude made a little cup with his hands and let some of the water pour into the makeshift dish.

"Here boy," Jude nodded toward the water. He tried to keep the bottle from sliding away. The dog looked like he was grinning at Jude and thumped his tail once, twice, three times but ignored the water and Jude's hands.

"Here," Jude said and jiggled his hands. The dog sniffed at them, then moved its head away.

"Aren't you thirsty?" Jude brought the little cup to the dog's mouth but by the time it got there most of the water had fallen out between the cracks in his fingers.

He tried again. After three tries, the dog found the water. It lapped it up in two swallows and whined. Jude filled his hands again and again. He could refill his water bottle in the morning. It was too dark to try to find the river now and the dog could get a better drink then too. If he stayed the night. Jude hoped he would really hard.

The dog had laid down on the pine branches nearby and Jude curled onto his side, one hand on the dog's back. He couldn't believe the dog had found him. That was the last thing he thought before he drifted off to sleep again.

Chapter 19

Marion Langlois

Marion winced as she pulled herself up out of the narrow crevice she'd dived into. She could feel tiny pebbles and large pieces of dirt wedged into her palms but didn't bother to rub them away.

The cavern had become silent. Had she killed it? The image of the bat's sharp teeth so close to her face made her feel nauseous. The smell of its rancid breath still hung in the damp air. Marion felt vulnerable outside the hiding spot. She shifted her weight, her head throbbing hard.

She'd sliced the bat hard in the face. But had it been enough to kill it or at least wound it badly enough to incapacitate it? And what about the other two...where were they? Marion started to shiver. Was it a response to the chilly air in the cavern, or the thought that other giant bats loomed above her somewhere, waiting in the dark for her to crawl out of her hiding spot?

If she were alone on this mountain, Marion would stay here. She'd deal with the horrible, pressing rock walls of the tight space and wait it out. But Rick was out there defenseless. Who knew how long those torches would stay lit or the fire would burn without her to tend to it.

Marion's gaze swept the rocky landscape of the cavern. She pointed her flashlight here and there, especially toward the ceiling. Nothing. She didn't see anything out of place. No sinister beady eyes watched her. There was no hissing or the now-familiar sound of bat wings chuffing in the air.

People called Marion a planner and she didn't shirk away from the title. She was organized to the point of anal and liked it that way. But in this case, she didn't have a plan. What the hell was she going to do? Stuck underground with psycho man-eating bats on the loose—Marion struggled to keep her emotions in check. She wanted to scream and sob and burst into hysterical laughter all at the same time.

Oh, God. Oh God, please get me out of here. Marion swiped a dirty hand over her eyes and took a few deep breaths. She stood motionless and waited for her breathing to return to normal. Panic was not her friend. And acting rashly could get her hurt, or worse.

What did she need? To get back to Rick. That was the priority. And no stupid bat—however big—was going to stop her. Right?

The pep talk failed as soon as Marion lifted her head in slow increments over the side of the shortest boulder. She peered over the side of the big stone and felt her heart sink like a brick. One of the big bats was perched on another stone nearby. It sat motionless, guarding her. Its eyes were red. Marion shrank back unconsciously against the big stone. The bat swept the area thoroughly from its perch, seeming to scan the rocks for signs of movement.

Marion waited until it was turned in the other direction to do her own rapid scan. She couldn't see the other one, either of them. Maybe the injured one really was dead. Or maybe it had flown off and the other one had gone with it? Marion ducked her head as the bat's head swiveled back toward her.

Trying to keep her breathing regular, Marion focused on possible next steps and tried to block out the myriad of possibilities, horrible endings to this scenario. But it was too hard. The images kept coming unbidden: Marion impaled by the bat's claws, the other two swooping in to bite into her; running to safety only to find the exit blocked by the missing bats. Or more of them swooping in. Who knew how many there were in all? She'd thought one was too hard to imagine, let alone four. And how long would it be before the whole colony returned?

Marion felt around behind her in the dark crypt-like space. There were lots and lots of rocks of different sizes. There was dirt. And not much else. She'd hoped maybe she'd find a branch that she could fashion into a spear using the knife. But that was stupid. Even if she could find a branch how long would it take to whittle the end into a sharp enough point? If there was even enough room in this tiny space. She pressed her lips together. *Think.* She had to think this through.

But she couldn't.

Instead, Marion sank back against the stones. Her body ached everywhere. Even her eyelids were sore. Maybe she could rest a little while. Maybe an idea would come to her if she stopped trying so hard to force it. Maybe—

A familiar hissing sound filled the cavern and bled down into Marion's hiding spot. Thoughts of resting and making a plan vanished. She had to do something—anything—and fast. Grabbing medium-sized rocks in both hands, Marion cautiously brought her head closer to the opening. When her eyes were clear of the hiding spot she threw the stones as hard as she could. Back down toward the center of the cavern where she and Rick and Jude had been earlier. The hissing broke off and then restarted.

But it was quieter. It was moving away. Marion poked her head up a little further and chanced a glance around. The red-eyed bat had flown off. She could barely see it in the dim light, circling and wobbling around in the empty air. It was fifty feet from her at least. She had to use this opportunity and get out of here. She grabbed the knife and slid it into the sheath on her leg, then grabbed another handful of smaller stones. Her breath was ragged as she launched herself out of the crevasse for a second time.

It had been easier falling in than getting out. And with her hands full, Marion couldn't get a grip on anything. The hissing grew louder once again. She glanced over her shoulder. The bat was making larger circles now, heading closer to Marion's hiding spot. She let all the stones fall except one. She kissed it and flung it toward the bat. She missed its head but hit one of the large wings. It made a pained screech and tipped to the left. Marion pulled herself up and out of the narrow trench of stone. She scrabbled upward, toward the top of the cavern, where she'd come in. For a few seconds, she felt a little ray of hope building in her chest. The cavern was quiet and Marion thought she'd done it. That she was free.

But the hissing started again. This time it was louder than before.

Marion looked over her shoulder and gasped. The bat was close. She ducked. The tip of its fibrous wing touched the back of one of her arms. She remained in a crouch, picked up another stone, and waited. The bat circled. Its red eyes made it look demonic. And its open mouth made it look terrifying.

Steady. Steady. Marion remembered a war movie she'd watched with Rick once. "Not until you see the whites of their eyes!" the commander had shouted. She held now, motionless until she saw the sharp, white teeth of the bat. Then she threw the rock as hard as she could. This time it hit its mark. The stone cracked against the razor-edged teeth in the wide mouth. The bat made a screaming noise and fell to the stones lining the cavern wall. It wasn't dead. That would be too easy Marion knew. But it had bought her time, maybe a minute or more. The hissing, screeching continued. Stones were knocked loose. She pictured it turning over, trying to get its bearings. It struggled against the rocks just on the other side of her. Marion's heart ricocheted off of the wall of her chest. She struggled upward as fast as she could.

It was treacherous and slow-going. Her hands slipped and slid on the damp stones, cuts, and nicks in her skin screamed at her whenever she grabbed at a rock or boulder to pull herself up. Everything in her wanted to look back, see where the bat was. But she didn't. Just listened over the sound of her panting breath for the hissing sound.

Her legs burned. Her feet, aching in the makeshift slippers, felt bruised and throbbed with every step. But she couldn't hear anything—no hiss, no screech—telling her the bat was in pursuit.

Above her, maybe six feet away was the opening where she'd come in. Where she and Jude had dragged Rick hours before. Marion focused her attention on it. Pulling herself upward, she realized her right foot was snagged.

Hurry. Hurry. Hurry.

The bandage on that foot had come loose. A long trail of

127

the canvas fabric was caught between two stones. Marion didn't bother trying to get it loose, just jerked her foot upward. Instead of a tearing sound and freedom though, her foot didn't budge. The material was too strong. Marion's hands shook as she frantically tried to free the filthy, greasy-feeling cloth. A knot that had caught between two sharp stones tightly wedged together. Marion panted, the sound too loud in the quiet cavern.

Come on. Come on!

Still stuck. Marion groaned and ripped frantically at the fabric on her foot with both hands. Her broken fingernails dug uselessly at the exposed knot. Sweat trickled down her forehead, a single bead hung on the end of her nose.

The knife!

Marion was about to slip it out when the material snapped beneath her. She hadn't anticipated the motion and couldn't correct her balance fast enough and fell to the left. Putting her hands out instinctively, she caught herself on a boulder seconds before crashing into it. The flashlight went flying. She smelled dank earth and the musty smell of enclosed spaces as she yanked herself upright. Where was the light? She couldn't wait and moved toward the opening above her.

She climbed, hand over hand. Almost there. So close. Nearly—

The last hand she put up closed over something sinewy and sharp. Marion gasped, jerked her head upward.

Above her stood one of the giant bats. Its claws were wound over a stone as it guarded the exit. This one had regular-looking eyes peering out of its ugly wrinkled gray face. It opened its mouth and screeched. Marion felt as though she'd been physically shoved. Along with the ear-splitting cry, something moved through the air and hit her with a jarring force.

Electricity jolted her system—the same feeling as before only magnified. Her arms and legs went numb. She yelled as she lost her footing. Slipping and sliding downward, Marion managed to jab her hands out on the end of wooden arms and grip onto the side of the wall. But she wouldn't be able to hold on long. Already, her grip on the stones was loosening. Marion looked in horror as her hands started sliding. First in centimeters, then inches.

No, no, no.

The bat had moved closer to the edge of the ravine, watching her descent, her slide down the side of the cavern's wall with interest. It knocked a large stone loose with its talons and it bounced down the ravine before it hit her side. Marion cried out but all that came from her mouth was a wheezy gasp. She clung to the rocks, terrified of falling. She felt herself slipping.

Please, please, please.

Please, God, help me.

Another inch, then another. Her greasy, cold hands slid over the stone. She couldn't feel the pain in her cut and bruised hands anymore at least. Was this how it would be when they got her? If she was paralyzed, would she still feel their teeth when they started to eat her? A choked sob rose from somewhere. It took Marion a second to realize it had come from her.

The bat picked its way down the stones toward her. Marion watched its progress. She was frozen in place, barely clinging to the dirty rocks. Would it sink its talons into the backs of her hands or give another of those pulses, sending her down to the bottom of the cavern? Her arms shook hard. Her legs were numb but began to tingle. Maybe the feeling was coming back.

The bat came closer. Two more steps, then three. It peered at her, cocked its ugly head. It was just feet away now. Its large wings were folded into teepees. It held these loosely at its sides.

Three feet.

Two.

One.

Marion closed her eyes momentarily as it reared its head back. It bared its teeth, then opened its mouth wide. Another hiss filled the air, loud. Louder than any of the others before. Marion could feel the hot stink of its breath coat her face. She wedged herself between two large stones, used her left leg to keep her in place. The strange paralysis was wearing off. Marion could feel her toes again, her arms and legs and hands.

Without hesitating, she reached down and pulled the knife free of its sheath. And then with every bit of strength, she had left, Marion plunged it upward.

Chapter 20

Rick Langlois

Apale gray-blue patch of sky was the first thing Rick saw when he opened his eyes. He pushed himself upright, moaning as he did so. His leg had burned last night. This morning it felt as though someone was jabbing hot nails into the burning flesh. When he lowered his head, waited for the dizziness to pass, he smelled something bad. Like rotten meat. Rick's stomach twisted and roiled. He waited a few seconds for the nausea to pass. He should drink something, was probably dehydrated. He fumbled around him for the water bottle and uncapped it, but then turned his head away. He couldn't swallow. He couldn't even open his mouth. It felt glued together, his dry lips welded shut.

Lifting a weak hand to his face, he felt three days' growth of beard itching his cheeks. His eyes felt sunken in his head. His entire side hurt but his leg...the pain in his leg was excruciating. He was hot again and felt the damp, itchy tracks of fresh sweat running down his scalp and back and chest. His breath wheezed slightly in his chest.

What was he going to do, he wondered almost dreamily. It was strange. Like he was watching this happen to a

character in a movie. He felt concerned about the Rick on
the ground, struggling to remain sitting upright. But he also
felt disconnected from him. Oh well, he thought as the man
slumped back over onto the makeshift bed. I guess he's not
getting up.

He drifted away, darkness stealing over him.

When he woke next, a sharp, persistent pain throbbed in
his head. *Dehydration*, his brain screamed. He tried to find
the water bottle again, but couldn't. His fingers felt big and
fat like someone had strapped sausages to the ends of his
hands. That same strange out-of-body experience was still
there. Rick felt an odd desire to laugh as he struggled to
right himself and then tipped backward. He should uncover
his leg, look at the wound. He should drink something. He
should…but everything was too hard. Too much effort. Rick
only wanted to sleep again, escape into the sweet oblivion of
unconsciousness.

He shook his head in slow motion.

No. That wasn't a good idea. He'd die out here. The coyotes
would come back and get him. If the infection in his body
didn't.

He needed…something. But what? A helicopter. A hospital.
No, that wasn't it. Well. He did need those things but there
was something else that skittered on the fringes of his brain.
It darted into his thoughts but then back out too fast for him
to catch it.

Rick finally managed to pull himself into a sitting position.
He grimaced as he pulled back the tape on the bandage on his
leg. The smell coming from it made him gag. He turned his
head away just in time to vomit. But there was nothing in his
stomach so he only dry heaved weakly a few times. His body

started to slide back down to the makeshift mat, but he forced himself to stay upright. He had to see it. Figure out what to do.

He looked back to his leg. The wound was infected. That was obvious. The gouges where the bat's claws had sliced into his skin had gone in deep. The whole area throbbed with his heartbeat. The holes were reddish-purple. Crusted blood was all around them. But worse, there was whitish green stuff—

Rick turned his head away again and covered the spot back up with the bandage without looking at it. He knew now, what he was dealing with. No need to stare at it. His head spun in a few dizzying circles while he tried to get his breathing back to normal.

He'd always hated blood. His own anyway. Hunting and dressing animals was different. But seeing his own blood or Jude or Marion's...he gagged reflexively.

It was infected. Very infected. He needed something to get it under control. He was burning up with fever. His body had fought hard but Rick didn't know how much longer it could continue. Not long, probably. Part of him felt relief at the thought. The pain might be over. But then, he realized and nearly giggled, then he'd be dead.

That thought sobered him.

Jude needed him. Marion...he wanted to fix things with Marion. He missed her. How easy they used to be together. Before...

Two birds jabbered loudly from trees across from each other and Rick wanted to cover his ears. They were deafening. Was this the fever too? Everything seemed exaggerated: the sounds in the forest, the heat in his body, the smell of infection.

Looking around himself, Rick searched for a branch to help

him stand. He needed to get upright. Find something to disinfect the wound, at least until help came. He might lose his leg. Lose his family...Where were Marion and Jude? Rick closed his eyes and shook his head gently. They hadn't been there during the night. Were they—

No.

No, they couldn't be dead. Maybe out there in the woods somewhere. Running to get him help. Or maybe needing help themselves. Needing him. Rick had to find a way out of here. He couldn't give in to the fever, to the weakness anymore. Moving felt like it might kill him. Again, he felt that weird giggle rising in his chest.

He struggled to his feet, clutching onto the big pine tree. When he was standing, he held onto the lowest branch, using it like a toddler holds a parent's hand to get him away from the little camp. The fire was barely smoldering. He'd need to feed it, make sure it didn't go out. But first, he had to find something to clean the wound out. The thought of the pain that was going to cause almost made him fall again, but he gripped the branch tighter. If he could do that he'd be more clear-headed, more himself. Instead of this, his head felt full of stuffing, limbs, and tongue and eyes thick and heavy and lethargic. And his leg and side shot full of burning hot lava.

Rick squinted. He'd spent enough time in the woods with his father hunting to know the basics of survival. And enough time with his grandmother who eschewed medicine for herbs to have a few ideas of what to look for.

Wild garlic would work. It was both an antibiotic and an antiseptic. Rick felt stupidly proud to remember that. What else? Ramps, or wild onions, might too, in a pinch. It was usually pretty easy to find the garlic in meadows and near roadsides. But could he find it here? Rick looked around him, head wobbling. There was a small clearing between the large pine tree where he stood and the big cavern about fifty feet away. Tall grasses blew in a faint breeze and a handful of wildflowers swayed. There was Queen Anne's lace, he recognized its white frilly head and a purple flower that looked like an oversized daisy...what was it called again?

Rick yanked on the pine branch under his hands but it didn't break. There was a downed branch nearby though. He veered in that direction dragging his bad leg. Every step made lightning bolts of pain race up and down it. He gasped at first, then clamped his teeth together.

He picked up the branch, moving in slow motion, and used it as a cane to help him move forward. He was so slow. But he was moving. Closer to the purple flowers. Purple coneflower that was it. It was also called...echinacea. What was it good for? He remembered his grandmother had liked it, gathering it fresh every summer in her harvesting basket. His head pounded hard. He needed water. Wait, what had he been trying to remember? Echinacea. It was good for colds. Fever? It was an immunity booster. That was it. If it helped with your immune system then it would work for infections, wouldn't it? Rick stared at the plant. What part was he supposed to use? Rick couldn't remember. Another miscellaneous fact popped into place: it was used to treat spider and snake bites. Where he'd learned that he didn't know. But he grabbed a fistful of the plant—three flowers, some stalks, and lots of the green leaves, then slowly, painfully retreated to his pallet.

Rick grunted at the pain as he lowered himself back onto the pallet. He found the water bottle and drained it, even though his stomach still felt ready to throw anything up that he put into it. Maybe he could make a liquid from the leaves and stalks and flowers? Then he could rinse out the wounds…but he had no pot and couldn't see another water bottle nearby.

He closed his eyes and pictured his grandmother in her tiny kitchen, in the little cabin she'd lived in. She hadn't been a traditional milk-and-cookies grandmother. Instead, she'd been more of a gypsy, wild and unfettered. Rick's father had had other names for her, not as flattering. But Rick pictured her moving between the piles of plants on the counter and the stove, to the table where clean, brown glass jars stood like soldiers.

"Like this," she said to Rick in his imagination. And she grabbed the leaves of the echinacea, grinding it in the mortar and pestle that she'd inherited from her grandmother.

So, he mashed the plant up in his mouth until it resembled a paste and spit it back out. It tasted slightly bitter and very green. He forced himself to swallow it, gagged, and nearly threw up again. But after waiting a few long seconds, his stomach settled. A fly buzzed around his head but Rick was too tired to shoo it away. He chewed again, grinding more of the plant with his mouth, then spit it out.

The next part would have to be done quickly. Rick wasn't sure if he could do it without passing out. Untacking the bandage from his leg again, he spread the green goo of herbs on the wound. The pain sliced through every nerve ending until Rick felt dizzy with it. The herbs felt sticky and thick. But he kept applying the paste until his hand was empty.

He closed his eyes then. Just for a minute, he thought. But he could already feel the darkness pulling him under. The sun was higher in the sky, he realized, and stained the backs of his eyelids orange. What time was it? Maybe nine o'clock? Ten?

He couldn't sleep now. Heavily, he pushed himself upward. His mouth tasted disgusting. He wanted water. The pack nearby had been emptied and the supplies were strewn around. Rick saw something orange. At first, he thought it was fruit, his mouth watered—or tried to—in anticipation. But it turned out to be the bottom of Marion's water bottle. He pulled it close. It felt full and he opened it, took two more big swallows. The water was warm and smelled slightly musty but his throat and mouth felt better afterward. What else was here? Some clothes and a few empty wrappers from ibuprofen. Rick remembered suddenly the bitter liquid that Marion had forced into his mouth. That explained it.

Rising slowly to his feet, Rick hobbled to the fire. He used the branch as a cane in one hand, the other clamped over the bulging bandage to keep the herbs from sliding out. When he got to the fire, he crouched slowly, like a very old man on his good leg, and fed the last of the dry branches into the fire. Finally, the wood caught.

Good. That was good. Rick felt his eyes closing again but forced them open with several strong blinks. He couldn't. Shouldn't sleep now. He should look for more medicine, something to eat. But the thought of walking around the meadow, searching for wild garlic, or eating more of the echinacea plant was exhausting.

He'd rest. Just for a few minutes by the fire. Wood. He'd need more of that too. Rick maneuvered himself awkwardly into a sitting position by the fire and let his chin rest on his chest. Just a few minutes...

Chapter 21

Jude Langlois

"Well, I'll be damned." A voice, low and growly woke Jude from a deep sleep. He jerked upright and looked around him wildly.

An old man stood a few feet away. He had a tangled gray beard and wore a dirty fishing hat, his hands rested on a gnarled but shiny-smooth walking stick. The dog next to Jude gave a yip and bolted upright. Then he danced around in tight little circles, continuing to yip as he lowered his head, ears pinned back. Beanie used to do that when he'd done something bad, Jude thought, like getting into the trash.

"So, you're not dead after all," the man said and snapped his fingers. The dog ran to his side and lay down, thumping his tail on the ground but not looking at the man. Jude stared, not realizing his mouth was open until a little drool ran out of the side of it. He wiped it on the back of his hand and shut his mouth.

"Who are you?" Jude asked.

"I was about to ask you the same thing," the man said. "Who are you and what are you doing out here? With my dog?"

"I—"

"Can't believe it," the man said, taking his hat off and slapping it against his leg twice before he replaced it. The dog jumped, startled, then went back to cowering. Why wasn't the man happier to see his pet, Jude wondered. And why was his dog so scared of him?

"I'm Jude." His voice squeaked a little at the end of the sentence. "Uh, Jude Langlois. My parents and I were…were hiking and got lost. I mean, I got lost. Can you help me get back to the campground?"

"Camping huh?" the man turned and spat, then jerked his chin toward Jude. "Where'd you lose your folks?"

A little voice in Jude's head told him not to tell this man too much. He was a stranger after all. But another part of Jude was so glad to see another human—and what looked like a woodsman who could probably help him get back to civilization—that he ignored the voice.

"We were camping at Osmore Pond and went, er, hiking. Up to Mount Crag. But my dad got hurt and my mom…she had to stay with him. So, I went to go get help."

The man's whistle interrupted Jude. "You're out here all on your own?"

Jude nodded, feeling a prickling heat spread through his stomach and chest.

"And you got here from Osmore Pond? That's a long ways from here."

"How far?"

The man raised his bushy eyebrows and shook his head. "Five miles I'd guess, if not more."

Five miles? Jude thought back to the climb he and his parents had made. It had felt long. But not that long.

"Could you, uh, take me there? Help me find the ranger?

139

Or warden or whoever? I need to let them know that my dad needs help."

The man squinted at Jude, his head tipped back slightly. His eyes were dark and the floppy hat shadowed them further.

"Well, now, I'm not too sure. Truth is, I'm not supposed to be in these woods. Warden don't like me much, ranger neither. Me or Turd."

It took a few seconds for Jude to realize the man meant the dog.

"Turd? That's your dog's name?"

The man knocked the dog's side lightly with his walking stick. Jude's hands curled into fists.

"That's his name. On a good day anyhow."

"What's yours?"

The man looked at him and squinted. "You can call me Tim."

"All right. Mister, uh, Tim, can you help me?"

Part of Jude hoped he'd say no. He'd probably be better off alone than with this weirdo. But then he thought about how scared he'd been the night before Scout showed up—Jude had thought that's what the dog's name should be—and was just as hopeful that Tim would say yes.

The man's mouth was turned downward. He rubbed a hand over his cheek and chin. It made a rough, scratching sound. Then he sighed and glanced from Scout to Jude and back again.

"I reckon I can get you close enough to the campground."

"Thank you," Jude said, already standing up and grabbing to shove things back into his pack. It was still damp and the fire was burned out, just a thin trail of smoke still coming out of the ashes. "Let me just put out the fire and I'll be ready to go."

"Well. You're a regular Boy Scout, ain't ya?"

Jude pretended Tim meant it in a nice way and pushed dirt

over the fire. Jude stomped down on it a few times, till no more smoke appeared. Dad had shown him that. Jude felt a twist of fear in his chest. What were his parents doing right now? Jude's eyes started to fill with tears. He blinked hard, head turned away from Tim until he got himself under control.

"All set," he said. Tim started to walk back the way Jude had come the night before, toward the river.

"Is it that way?" he said and hesitated.

"Nope," Tim said. "But I need to refill my canteen and Turd probably needs a drink. If that's all right with you."

"Uh, sure. Of course. I'll refill my bottle, too."

Tim either didn't hear him or didn't care. He just kept walking until he was out of sight. Jude jogged after him, his pack banging uncomfortably on his back.

When he reached the riverbank, the dog was gleefully lapping water in an area where the water was quiet. Tim unleashed a banged-up metal canteen from under his jacket and let the river water fill it. The water was murky and brown and Jude was about to ask if Tim was sure he wanted to drink that when he saw the old man fish a little vial out of his pocket.

"Iodine tablets," he said and dropped two into the canteen before recapping it.

"Oh. I have a filtered bottle," Jude said as though Tim had offered him some. Tim ignored him and snapped his fingers toward Scout. The dog stopped drinking mid-lap and bounded to his master's feet.

"I like S...your dog," Jude said. "It was cool the way he found me last night."

"He's a stupid mutt, but he's a good tracker. When he's not off chasing rabbits."

"He's not stupid," Jude said, then blushed as he plunged his water bottle into the cold river. After it was full he capped it and put it into his pack. It took a little while for the filter system to work.

Scout was looking at Jude when he'd finished. When Jude smiled, the dog wagged its tail on the ground.

"Let's go," Tim said. "Keep up, huh?"

"Sure," Jude said. "Thank you again for—"

But Tim had already loped yards ahead and let the tree branches swing back into place, nearly catching Jude in the face. Jude hurried to catch up, hope sinking into his hiking boots. Had he done the right thing?

***

When they stopped almost an hour later, Jude was ready to fall over with fatigue. Keeping up with Tim was impossible. More than once, he'd been forced to call out, unable to find either the man or the dog in the thick woods.

"Keep up, would ya?" Tim had snarled the last time Jude had run to him, panting. Jude's legs wobbled and his arms shook. He was starving—his stomach had been growling for hours it seemed like—and thirsty.

"I need…a…drink," Jude had panted. Finally, Tim had relented, pausing under two big pine trees. Scout sniffed the ground incessantly, running first one way and then the other.

"What's he doing?" Jude asked after he'd caught his breath and drank a few big gulps of water.

"Tracking," Tim said. "He's not too bad at it. Can usually find me some good…" Tim glanced at Jude sideways. "Well. He can find any animals I tell him to out here. When he's not distracted by rabbits."

Jude nodded, took another sip of water. Some of it dripped down his chin. "That's cool. What do you like to hunt out here?"

Tim put his canteen back. "Nothing much," he said and snapped for the dog. Then, "Time to go."

"But—"

Tim was already gone. Jude hurried to cap his water bottle and stuff it back into his pack before crashing through the trees, once more in danger of losing sight of the man and his dog.

***

They stopped for "lunch" shortly after that break. Maybe Tim had gotten sick of hearing Jude complain about how hungry he was. Or maybe he was just ready to eat. Either way, Jude's mouth watered when Tim pulled a chunk of smoked salami from a dirty-looking cloth in his pack. He used a jackknife to cut off thick slices which he chewed with his mouth partly open. He didn't offer any to Jude but did toss a few pieces on the ground for Scout. Scout ate these without bothering to chew and kept his dark eyes on his master's hands.

Jude swallowed and looked away. He couldn't ask Tim for food, on top of everything else. But what kind of a mean person lets a kid starve to death while he shovels food in his face, Jude wondered.

He looked through his pack. He'd shared a granola bar with the dog last night. He had one left and one extremely bruised and squishy orange. Carefully, he tore the bar's wrapper with his teeth. A single chocolate chip fell out of the package and Jude caught it and shoved it into his mouth. The sweetness

143

melted on his tongue too fast. He gobbled the rest of the bar down in three bites, telling himself all the while to slow down, slow down, slow down. But he couldn't. He'd save the orange though, he decided, till later.

"How'd your father get hurt?" Tim asked.

"Huh? Oh, he uh...fell."

Tim stared at him unblinkingly. "Fell, huh?"

Jude nodded. Part of him wanted to tell Tim the whole story. A giant bat—who wouldn't want to tell that story?—but part of him felt weird about it. Anyway, Tim didn't seem like the kind of guy who'd believe in giant bats.

"You see anything else while you've been out here?"

Jude shook his head. "No. Well, we saw some bats."

Tim looked at him and he paused with a piece of meat halfway to his mouth. "Bats?"

"Yeah. A whole flock...no, they're called what again?" He thought about it.

"Colony."

"Yeah, that's it. We saw one of those."

"Where was this?"

"Down by the lake first. And then when we were up at the..." Jude swallowed hard. Oops. He hadn't meant to—

"Up at what?"

Jude swallowed. His throat felt dry.

"At the cavern." His voice was barely more than a whisper.

"What kind of cavern?" Tim's voice sounded normal but his eyes looked weird. Sort of hard and intense, the way Jude's grandmother did when she found sticky handprints on her freshly-washed kitchen cabinets.

"You know the regular kind. Like underground with lots of rocks...sort of like a cave but bigger."

"Uh-huh."

Tim was studying him now and had stopped chewing. Jude looked away, then glanced back. Tim was still staring.

"So, whereabouts was that?"

"Oh, uh, I'm not really sure. We were on our way to the top of Mount Crag," Jude lied. "But we didn't get there. We got, uh, lost a little."

"Lost a little?"

Jude nodded.

"I left from there to get help. I was going south but then I fell into the river."

Tim raised his eyebrows.

"And I got carried downstream a little."

"How many bats did you say you saw?" Tim asked casually, but he still stared at Jude intensely.

"There was a lot," Jude said. "Tons of them. And then—"

Tim smiled faintly. "Then what?"

"Nothing," Jude said. "Just…and then I took some pictures with my mom's camera." He finished weakly.

Tim was quiet as he cut another circle of the smoked meat off the stick and tossed it to Scout. The dog snapped it out of the air and swallowed.

"You think you could find where you fell in?" Tim asked.

Jude nodded in relief. He was glad Tim was done asking about the bats. A sudden thought occurred to Jude.

"Do you have a radio?"

"Huh?" Tim stopped chewing.

"A radio. To call for help for my dad." Jude felt stupid. He should have asked sooner.

"Oh sure, a radio," Tim said slowly. "Yeah, I've got one. But it won't work here. I need to be up higher to use it. Out of the tree coverage," he pointed with his knife blade at the dense forest.

"Oh." Jude felt a little shimmer of hope dance in his chest.

"Tell you what," Tim wiped the knife blade on the dirty cloth and put everything back into his pack. "How about we find your folks? I'll radio from there to get help. What do you say?"

Jude swallowed hard. He could still taste a little of the sweet granola in his throat. On the one hand, he wanted to go back to the campground and find the ranger. They had to be just a couple of miles away now. On the other, he wanted to see his parents, wanted to hug his mother more than anything. And he was still bringing help, wasn't he?

"Okay," he said. "I can show you where I fell in. But I don't know how we'll find it from there. I lost my compass—"

"Don't need one," Tim said. "Come on, let's go."

Chapter 22

Marion Langlois

The bowie knife connected with the bat's neck in a sickening crunch. Marion felt stuff moving around where the blade had gone in—tendons, muscles—before it crunched against bones. The bat jerked and she lost her grip on the knife's handle. She stared transfixed as the bat's open-mouthed hiss turned into a strangled gasp. Then its body tipped like it was moving in slow motion. It fell forward, directly toward Marion. Its jagged teeth were open wide, black oozy stuff—blood?—gushed out of the wound in its neck.

Marion put her arms up instinctively to block her head and face. But the bat crashed into her and sent her tipping backward. For a single second, Marion thought, I'll be all right. I'm okay. But the weight of the bat's body and her already precarious hold pitched her backward. She screamed as both she and the bat flew backward into the darkness below.

Miraculously, Marion's fall was halted by a smooth, flat rock. Positioned at just the right angle, it stopped her freefall, almost cradling her in a nook worn smooth by a dripping stone directly overhead. Marion lay there letting the cool drips falling on her chest. She was okay, she realized in amazement. Minus the bumps, bruises, and cuts she wasn't much worse off than when she'd first entered the cavern.

The knife was Marion's next thought. She sat up, tested her footing, and found it solid. The big bat's crumpled body lay lower down and slightly to the right. One of its wings was torn, a sharp stone poking up through it. The other was partially spread, hiding its neck and the knife. At least, Marion hoped the knife was still there.

She squatted a foot from the bat's body. Was it dead, she wondered, or waiting for her to get close so it could strike again? She put out a hand toward it, then drew it back. Her breathing was loud in the quiet space and her legs shook.

Just do it fast. Like a Band-Aid. But still, she hesitated. Putting her hand out again, she allowed it to hover over the bat. Then she slowly lowered it toward the thing's wing.

"Hey, she said, her voice hoarse. "Are you dead, bat?"

It didn't move.

"I'm getting my knife now. Don't you dare bite me if you're still alive."

She lowered her hand another two inches.

"Bat?"

Nothing.

Marion lowered her hand closer. It was just a few inches away now. She could almost feel the thick wing. It smelled awful—musty and rancid—and she turned her head away for a lungful of fresh air.

Two inches now.

One inch.

Marion put her fingertips on its wing. It wasn't as leathery as it looked. It felt much lighter than she'd expected, more like taut silk than leather. She shivered and pushed the wing in. Or tried to. Instead, it popped back out and then closer to the bat's body. Beneath it though, she was sure she'd seen the silver band of the knife between the handle and the blade. She pushed the wing again.

There it was. The bowie knife was still stuck firmly in the bat's neck. Marion swallowed and rested her hand lightly on the handle. It was warm and smooth under her bloodied, sticky skin. Pressing her lips together, Marion gripped the handle and started to pull.

The blade eased out, a centimeter at a time. It made a horrible sucking sound when it started to move. She'd wipe the blade clean on her pants when it was free. Put it back into the leg sheath. And then get the hell out of here.

It was nearly out. But the bat's head moved suddenly. It snarled and hissed, making a choking sound as it did so. Then it snapped its teeth. They brushed the side of her hand. She yelped, pulled the knife out the rest of the way, and slashed at its head again with the blade.

There was a sickening moment when Marion thought she'd miss. But she didn't. This time, she took off its head. More of the black stuff came out and the head hung to one side like a disjointed doll. Its eyes bulged a little and its talons and wings twitched. Marion clutched the knife close to her pounding heart and watched for any other sign of movement.

But there was nothing.

She waited a few minutes more. *Please, please, please be dead.* No movement.

Marion cleaned the blade, never taking her eyes off of the bat. She waited for it to come back to life, for its head to reattach itself and lunge at her. But it remained where it was.

Finally, she stuck the knife back into the sheath and climbed up the side of the cavern's wall once more.

***

It took more than an agonizing hour to get back out of the cavern. Marion made a wrong turn once, only realizing it after she'd come across a tiny waterfall. She'd had to retrace her steps and then stumbled and crawled the rest of the way. Finally, the tunnel spit her out into the little clearing. She wanted to run to check on Rick and the fire, but could barely stand upright. Her legs screamed for a rest. Her back and neck and head all throbbed along with her heartbeat. She was more tired than she'd ever been in her life.

But Marion saw the fire—it was still burning!—and the scattering of clothes around their little campsite. She looked to where she'd left Rick resting, but the low-hanging limbs of the big pine hid him from view.

She stumbled forward. Most of one of the canvas shoes had fallen off in the cave, leaving her left foot almost fully exposed. Marion kept her eyes where she'd left Rick as she crossed the clearing. She was nearly there when she spotted the tracks. Dog prints. Lots and lots of them. She could see them clearly in the dry, sandy areas underneath the pines not far from their little camp.

"No. No. No." Marion chanted the word like a mantra and swallowed hard. She lost count at more than thirty prints.

"Rick?" She called out, but her voice was nothing more than a weak croak. "Rick, are you okay?"

She continued forward. Hoped to see her husband just as she'd left him. On his makeshift cot, feverish and too-pale but alive. Just a few more feet and she'd be able to see under those branches.

There.

She could just make out the edges of the little bed of pine boughs and clothes.

But it was empty.

"Rick?" she croaked again. A soft breeze teased at the hair around Marion's face. "Rick?"

There was no answer.

She walked in jerky steps to the bed and collapsed near it. She patted the clothes stupidly, as though her husband might be hiding in them.

"Rick?"

He was dead. Marion put her head between her knees and let the tears come finally. He was gone. Rick was gone. Her brain kept feeding her the information she couldn't accept it. *The coyotes must have come back,* a little voice in her brain patiently explained. *They must have...*she couldn't think about it. Rick was gone. *Gone. Gone.*

She sobbed but no more tears came from her eyes. She was too dehydrated, she realized idly. She should drink something. Instead, she let gravity pull her down onto the little bed. The bad, sour smell of sickness mixed with the fresh, piney smell of the needles underneath her. She lay there, stared out at the landscape without seeing any of it.

She needed to get up. Maybe Rick wasn't dead. Maybe the coyotes had only dragged him off. She could still find him, run them off. But first, she had to get off the ground and—

"Marion?" Rick's voice called. Marion blinked. Oh God, she was going crazy now on top of everything else.

"Marion?"

That was a real voice, wasn't it?

Marion shoved herself upright, her arms trembling, and scanned the clearing, then the woods beyond it.

Something leaned against a tree nearby.

"Rick?" She breathed.

"I'm sorry, I—"

She launched herself at her husband, grabbed him so hard that they both nearly tipped over backward.

"Rick?" She laughed and held his gaunt face in both her dirty, dried-blood hands. "I thought you were dead. I thought—" she broke off and kissed his nose, his eyes, his cheeks. She couldn't stop laughing. *I'm hysterical,* she thought. *I'm losing it.* But it didn't seem to matter to Rick. He sagged heavily against the tree. His blue eyes were bloodshot in his too-white face. He smiled at her or tried to but it turned into a grimace.

"You're not dead," she said. "You're—"

"I'm okay," he said, his voice so soft she had to lean toward him so she wouldn't miss anything. "Where's Jude?"

Marion's smile faded and the silly laughter dried up in her chest.

"Jude's...gone." She saw his face and quickly corrected herself. "I mean, he left. He went to go get help, while we were sleeping. He left us a note—"

"Gone? Alone?" Rick whispered and closed his eyes.

Marion nodded. "Come, sit down. I'll tell you everything."

Rick leaned on her and a branch for support. It took them several long minutes to make it back to the little camp and a few more painful-sounding ones for him to settle back down onto the pallet of clothes.

Marion told Rick everything, speaking slowly because he seemed dazed and kept interrupting to ask her questions that she'd already answered. After she was done he squeezed her hand gently.

"I thought you were both—" He took a ragged breath. "I don't know what I'd do if anything happened to you, Marion...or Jude."

"Nothing is going to happen to either of us. Jude is a smart boy. He is fine, I know it. We need to figure out what to do next. But right now you need to rest."

"I was...getting firewood." His breath wheezed in and out and his eyelids fluttered.

She put a hand to his forehead. That's what was different. He wasn't burning hot anymore. And there was no slick of sweat across his face.

"It looks like the fever broke," she said.

"...think so. Found some...flowers."

Flowers? Marion frowned but kept her hand on his chest. It too seemed to have shrunk in the short time they'd been out here.

"Just rest now," Marion said. "And when you wake up, we'll go and look for Jude."

But Rick was already sleeping, his mouth partially open.

Chapter 23

Jude Langlois

I f Jude never went into the woods again it would be okay with him. He was sick of looking at tree branches and tripping over rocks and roots. His feet and legs felt raw and tender, the same way his teeth did after a visit to the dentist. He sucked in a breath as a branch swung back and nearly hit him in the face.

Again.

Scout seemed to sense his discomfort. He ran back and forth between Tim and Jude, licked Jude's hand occasionally, or circled him wagging his tail. It was almost like he was telling Jude, "Good job! Keep it up." Then he'd dart back up to where Tim was.

Jude's stomach had gone from growling to pinching and hurting. He'd never been so hungry. Once, his friend Thomas's youth group had done a no-eating challenge. For thirty hours, no one ate—not the kids or the youth group leaders—to experience what it was like to starve. Jude and Thomas hadn't been old enough to participate and Jude had been secretly glad. Not eating hadn't sounded like much fun. Now he knew for sure that it wasn't.

"...further now." Tim's voice was almost lost through the thick undergrowth of the forest.

"What?"

Tim stopped, waited for Jude to catch up. Jude was practically panting but Tim didn't seem bothered by the steep uphill climb.

"I said it's not much further now. Or shouldn't be if you got your facts straight."

Jude nodded but his stomach twisted uncomfortably. Had he gotten his facts straight? He'd led Tim where he'd thought he'd come out of the river. Tim had then gone to a place further downstream where they had crossed. The water there had been only knee-high, for Tim at least, thigh-high for Jude. Then they'd walked back upriver. Tim had wanted to know the exact spot where Jude had gone in to make tracking his path backward easier. They'd spent a lot of time looking along the riverbank. Tim had been looking for tracks, bent branches, something that would point to Jude's entry point, but had finally given up.

Instead, they'd guesstimated from where Jude thought he'd fallen in. And since then, Jude had been following Tim like a lost puppy.

He was sick of it. He was exhausted and starving and he missed his parents. He wished he'd never left them. That they'd never taken this stupid trip at all. They could be safely at home now. Mom would be in her art studio—really just a spare bedroom—where she drew and painted or working in her flower garden. Jude would be playing with a friend or a video game. Dad would be at work. He thought about it and felt a different kind of hunger inside. The hunger for regular, normal life. He missed his soft bed and pillows and the glow-in-the-dark planets and stars on his ceiling. He missed the smell of his bedroom and the other scents of home: the clothes dryer smell, food cooking in the kitchen, the scent of grease and metal that was permanently stuck on Dad's clothes and hands.

"...that?" Tim had stopped and Jude nearly ran into him. He caught himself before he did, then stepped back a few feet.

Jude listened but he couldn't hear anything.

"What?"

Tim sniffed the air. "You can't smell that?"

Jude sniffed. He smelled the same thing he'd been smelling for hours: pine needles and dried up dead leaves and occasionally, some flowery smell.

"Nope."

"Woodsmoke."

Jude sniffed again. And then he could smell it too. Faintly, but it was there.

"What's that mean?"

"That someone else is close by."

"My parents?"

Tim shrugged. "Could be. We're going the right way."

"How can you tell?"

"I've been following your tracks."

"You have? You found them?"

Tim gave a single nod. "Back there a way. Let's go,"

Jude felt hope bubble up in his chest. They were getting closer. He wanted to start calling out to his parents, wanted to push past Tim, and run the rest of the way there. Even though he had no idea how to find the way. His legs still felt like wooden baseball bats but he thought he could still run.

Instead, he hurried to catch up to Tim who once again, was

far in front. Scout bounded back, gave Jude a messy lick on the hand, and wagged his tail.

"You hear that, boy?" Jude said, quietly enough so that Tim wouldn't hear him. "We're almost there! My mom and dad will be so glad to see us. Well, you and me anyway." He whispered that last part. He didn't like Tim much and didn't trust him. Why was he so eager to find Jude's parents? It didn't seem like he cared much about Jude himself. Maybe it had something to do with the bats.

Scout ran back ahead and Jude thought about Tim and how he'd acted when Jude said that they'd seen a colony of bats. But who cared about bats? Was Tim some sort of scientist? He'd learned about them in school, the scientists who studied animals. No, not scientists. They were called something else… biologists. That was it.

Jude didn't know any, but somehow Tim didn't look like he was one of those. He looked more like a homeless person. Or a convict. Or at least, someone who wasn't official. He didn't wear a uniform or anything. And what had he said about the game warden? That he didn't like Tim. Why wouldn't he if they were working together? Didn't outdoor people all sort of work together and know each other?

Jude tripped on a root that was hidden under lots of green leaves and almost fell. He grabbed a nearby tree trunk at the last second. The rough bark scraped against his already raw palms. But even that didn't discourage him. He was almost there. He could already feel his parents' arms around him as they hugged him. Mom would probably cry and be angry at him, but underneath it, she'd been glad to see him. And Dad—

"Stop," Tim said, his voice a loud whisper. Again, Jude hadn't realized the old man had stopped walking and nearly run into him. "We're getting close."

Jude felt his heart glow in his chest. "That's awesome! Can I go first—"

"Shut up," Tim said and made a slicing motion near his neck. "We're not sure this is your parents' camp. Might be. Probably it is. But we can't be sure. I'm going to scout it out a little. You stay here."

"No way! I—"

"I'm not asking you." Tim's face, normally blank-bordering-on-grumpy now looked angry. "Sit down." Tim jabbed a finger toward a fallen tree. "And stay quiet."

"But I thought you said you'd been following my tracks—"

"Have been. Least, I think they're yours. But out here you never know who you might run into. Stay put."

Tim walked off into the brush. Within seconds Jude couldn't see him anymore. Scout sat by Jude's side until Tim snapped his fingers in the distance. Then the dog ran off and Jude was alone in the forest.

Again.

He wondered what Tim had meant: "Out here you never know who you might run into." Like hunters? Jude didn't think it was hunting season for anything now, not in the middle of summer. At least, not any animals they hunted. Dad took him hunting twice but the last couple of years he'd been too busy at work. His mother, who didn't even like hunting, had argued with Dad about it. Jude had come in from Peyton's house at the tail end of the conversation.

"All you ever think about is that damn garage," his mother had said, her voice so tight it sounded like a guitar string about to break.

"It's just a season, Marion. I need to set things up the right way, get everyone on the same page," Dad had said. His voice hadn't sounded so much angry as tired out. "It won't be like this forever."

"No, it won't," Mom had said.

"What do you mean by that?"

"I mean that I'm not going to—"

Then Jude had bumped into the kitchen chair which had squealed across the floor. Mom had come out of their bedroom seconds later and plastered a big, fake smile across her face. But it hadn't reached her eyes which looked a little puffy and red.

"Hi honey, we didn't hear you come in." She'd cleared her throat, walked over, and hugged him. She felt stiff, like a mannequin.

Jude bit his lip now. He wished he'd followed Tim. He didn't like being out here all alone. Even though Tim wasn't exactly nice or friendly, he was an adult. And he seemed to know what he was doing. What if Tim got lost? Or couldn't find Jude again after he went to scope things out?

Or what if he just left me here, Jude wondered. What if he doesn't need me anymore, so he abandoned me? Goosebumps ran up and down Jude's legs under his still-damp pants. What should he do?

Jude stood up. He wasn't going to get left behind. And he wasn't going to sit out here like a stupid baby, waiting for Tim to come back. They had to be close to Mom and Dad's camp now. Jude would just follow the smell of the wood smoke and find it himself.

But what if you get lost again, a little voice in his head asked. What then?

I won't, Jude thought. I just won't.

Chapter 24

Rick Langlois

Rick woke with a start. Marion's voice had been calling to him in his dream. Now, as he opened his eyes, he realized it hadn't been a dream at all. It took him a few seconds to put together where he was but when he remembered, he sat upright.

At least, he tried to. A groan came from his mouth as he clutched at his leg and side. He felt Marion's small, strong hands on his back helping to guide him up into a sitting position.

"Rick, there's someone there," Marion whispered, her mouth close to his ear. "I saw him in the trees."

Rick's heart leaped. His first thought was, *we've been rescued!* But his next was, *why would our rescuer be hiding in the woods?*

"Where?" he asked.

Marion pointed with a shaking finger toward a tangle of trees that were thickly hung with vines about a hundred feet from where they were sitting.

"I saw a flash of movement. I thought it was the coyotes, that they'd come back. But then I saw his silhouette. What's he doing out there?" Her voice was anxious and she looked nervously at the woods, eyes flicking over the trees.

"My pack. Where is it?"

Marion glanced at him, eyes wide.

"Get it."

She moved away from him. Rick kept his eyes trained on the woods. Maybe Marion had seen a shadow or change in the light and thought it was a man. He couldn't see anything moving—wait!

There.

He'd just seen a tree branch shake and then the flash of beige. Was it a person or a coyote?

Marion moved back to where she'd been standing, and lowered the pack to the ground silently. "What do you need?"

Rick winced as he shifted positions.

"Please tell me you brought a gun," Marion said.

He shook his head. "Didn't think I'd need it at the campground. But I always keep a bottle of bear spray in there. It's at the bottom in a little nylon bag with some other emergency supplies. Wish I'd thought to get it out before we'd gone into that cavern."

Marion pressed her lips together and dug through the pack. Rick kept his gaze on the trees. Seconds later, a man walked out, holding his hands up as though he were surrendering.

"Marion," Rick whispered.

She glanced from him to the woods.

"Oh," she said her voice a hoarse whisper. Rick struggled to his feet, using the cane with one hand and keeping the other clamped over the fierce burning pain in his leg. As though he could hold the pain in with his hand.

"I'm friendly," the man said, advancing a few more steps. Marion didn't stop digging in the pack and Rick was glad. He felt dizzy and off-centered.

"Just the same, friend, don't come any closer," Rick said. "My family and I have had a hell of a time these last few days. Little jumpier than we'd normally be."

The man cocked his head, stopped walking.

"You Jude's parents?"

Rick felt his heart jump in his chest at the same time Marion cried out. "Jude? Do you know where he is?"

The man nodded.

"He's fine."

"Oh thank God," Marion said. "We've been so worried—"

"No, thank me," the man replied. "It was me that saved him out there in the woods. Found him in the nick of time. Just before he went over the side of a cliff."

Marion made a strangling sound.

"Where is he?" Rick asked.

"He's nearby," the man replied. "I wanted to be sure what I was dealing with here before I brought a young boy into the mix."

"Go get him," Marion said, her voice two octaves higher than usual. "Please."

"Well now, I can do that," the man said. He pulled his floppy, dirty hat free and scratched his head once, then replaced it. "Thing is, I'm looking for some information myself. Thought we could do a little…exchange if you will."

"What kind of information?" Rick asked. He felt as weak as a baby bird but tried to make his voice stronger than it was. He ground the stick deeper into the ground to stabilize him.

"The boy said you'd seen a colony of bats up around here," the man's gaze darted around the clearing, came to rest on the big entrance of the tunnel. "Ah. That must be it."

Rick nodded. "What of it?"

"I'm hunting them."

"Hunting...what?" Marion asked. "Bats?"

The man gave a half-smile. "Yup."

"Why?" Marion asked.

He cocked his head, ran his eyes up and down Marion, and then Rick. "Looks like you two have had a tangle with a wild animal."

Marion and Rick didn't say anything.

"Where's Jude?" Marion asked again. "We want our son. Then we'll tell you everything you want to know."

The man sighed, looked down at the ground as though he were debating something. But when he looked up, he nodded.

"All right," he said. "I'll go get him."

"Wait," Rick said. "I'll go with you."

"Rick," Marion hissed. "You can't."

"I'm not letting him out of my sight," he said softly under his breath.

"Then let me go with him," Marion said. "I'll bring Jude back."

Rick shook his head. "I don't trust him," he whispered. "And I don't want anything happening to you."

"That's very sweet, but of the two of us right now I think I can better—"

"Did you find it?" Rick interrupted.

Marion hesitated, then nodded.

"Give it to me. Please, Marion, trust me."

She didn't move.

"Time's wasting," the man said in a singsong voice.

Finally, she slipped the can of bear spray into Rick's right pants pocket. He switched his grip on the stick to his left hand, then nodded at the man.

"What's your name?" Rick asked.

"Tim."

"Rick," Rick replied. "Now that we're on friendly terms… let's go."

Tim smiled, showing grayish teeth. He snapped his fingers. A dog bolted from the undergrowth to his side. Rick, startled by the movement nearly fell backward but caught himself on a nearby tree.

"This here's Turd," Tim said, and the dog whined and thumped its tail, staring at the ground. "Tracking dog. He'll lead you right to your son."

"What?" Rick said. "Where are you going?"

"I'm going to stay here with your wife. Get a little more information about the whereabouts of these bats."

"No. No way," Rick said. "Sorry, Tim, but I don't know you. And I'm not leaving you here with Marion. And who's to say that this dog will bring me anywhere close to our son and not off the side of a cliff?"

Tim made a tut-tutting sound. "Suspicious lot, aren't you?"

"I'll go," Marion said. The dog thumped his tail once and Marion squatted down, pet his head. "I have Jude's shirt," she looked up at the men. "Can he track it with that?"

"Oh sure," Tim said. "He's not good for much but he's a helluva tracking dog."

"Marion—" Rick said.

"What do I do?" she ignored Rick, her voice calm.

"Just give him a good sniff," said Tim. "Keep the shirt with you—he might need a refresher on the trail."

"How far away is he?"

Tim shrugged, gave another greasy smile. "Not too far.

Maybe twenty, thirty minutes."

"Thirty?" Rick said. "You left our boy out there alone, while you—"

"Come on, Rick," Tim said and moved toward the campsite. "Looks like you need to take a load off. I've got a radio here in my pack. What? Did I forget to mention that? Ah, the old memory's getting slippery."

Rick started to say something, but Tim cut him off.

"As soon as you tell me more about the bats, I'll let you use it. You can call for help. Get your family out of here. What do you say?"

Rick looked at Marion.

She gave a small nod. "It will be okay," she said and squeezed his forearm gently. "I'll be back with Jude soon. Tell him what he wants to know and let's get out of here."

Rick nodded.

"All right," he said to Tim. As Tim walked toward the camp he surveyed the cavern above them. The opening wasn't visible from where they were but Tim was tracing the rocks and scraggly brush with his eyes.

Rick slipped the bear spray into Marion's pocket. She frowned, shook her head.

"No, you keep it," she mouthed.

Rick shook his head. "Just hurry."

This time, she didn't argue.

Chapter 25

Jude Langlois

Jude rubbed his cheek as yet another branch whipped across his face. He was so tired now that it felt hard to move them out of the way. His hand came away sticky with pine pitch, the sap from the tree. He'd learned in history class that pioneers and maybe Native Americans used to chew it. Jude stuck some of it into his mouth, which was so dry it felt like it was full of flour. The taste was strong and kind of bitter. He spat the sap out. Maybe it was a different part of the tree you could chew.

He stopped walking and checked his surroundings again. This time, he was determined not to do anything stupid. He'd been carefully following the tracks of Tim. Jude looked for bent or broken branches and trampled down grasses. Occasionally he found a partial footprint in the earth where Tim's boot had touched dirt rather than the dry leaves that covered most of the floor of the woods. He had to be getting close. Didn't he?

The smell of smoke wasn't as strong now, but that could be because the breeze had shifted. Jude wanted to stop and rest. To eat the last mushy orange in his pack and drink some water.

But he pushed on.

It was hard to track in the woods. Jude's back ached from staying mostly bent over and his pack was digging even more uncomfortably into his shoulders. Still, Mom and Dad could be just minutes away now. He felt his heart squeeze in his chest before it went back to pounding hard. Sweat trickled in little itchy paths down his forehead but he'd stopped wiping it away a long time ago. It took too much effort.

The sound of something moving through the undergrowth stopped Jude in his tracks. He swept his eyes around him, first in one direction and then the other. What was it? It could be nothing. A squirrel. A chipmunk, he told himself. But it was too big for that. Suddenly he thought of the thing that he'd heard yesterday. The thing that had chased him. Was it here now? Was it going to leap from the bushes and—

A brown body bolted out of the dense undergrowth. Jude froze.

Scout yipped and ran to him. Relief flooded Jude's whole body. He sank to his knees and wrapped his arms around the dog.

"Hey boy, you found me," he said. "How'd you do that, huh?" He scratched behind Scout's ears and the dog paused in his panting to moan quietly. "What are you doing out here again?" The dog wagged its tail and resumed panting, his long, pink tongue taking an occasional swipe at Jude's hand and arm. "Did you come back for me?"

Jude's eyes started to fill with tears and he smeared them away on the dog's fur, hugging him tightly. Scout whined and wriggled until Jude let go. Then the dog sneezed, spraying Jude with a fine mist.

"Gross," Jude said, but he laughed. "Can you bring me back

to the camp?"

Scout cocked his head. Jude heard something else moving through the forest. He looked but couldn't see anything.

"What's that?" he whispered, keeping his hand on Scout's back. The dog whined once, then fell silent. Jude wiped the back of his hands slowly on his pants and stared at the trees.

There! Branches moved. He heard the sound of feet crunching over dry leaves and twigs on the forest floor. Maybe it was just Tim. Or maybe it was that thing—

A stooped-over figure came out from underneath a tight grove of pine trees. Like Jude, the person wiped away sticky pine sap.

"Dog?" a voice called. "Dog, where are you?" It was a woman's voice. And Jude knew it well.

"Mom! Mom, I'm here!" Jude cried, running toward his mother at the same time. She finally emerged from the tangle of pine branches. Her hair was snarled and had bits of bark and twigs in it. She was dirty and bruised and cut up. Jude rushed to her and fell into her arms.

"Jude, Jude, Jude," she breathed his name, half-laughing, and half-crying. She started to cry for real then. He felt hot tears rolling from her face onto his hair and down his neck as she held him close.

"Oh, my God, Jude. You're okay. Oh, thank God." She swayed, holding him tight, rocking him like he was a baby.

He loved every second of it.

Finally, after many long minutes, she let go. She put her hands on his arms and held him away from her, lowering her face to his.

"Are you okay, baby?"

He nodded. "Yeah, I'm okay. I was...I got lost. But then

Scout found me. And then Tim came along and—"

"He's with Dad now. We need to hurry and get back. I know you must have a lot to tell me, but you'll have to do it while we hike, okay?" Mom's voice was tight and pinched sounding, like when Jude had told her that he needed three-dozen cupcakes for school…the night before the bake sale.

Jude nodded. "Okay," he said. "Scout can lead us if you need him to. He's really good at it."

His mom nodded. "You named the dog Scout?" she asked, as she put her arm around his shoulders and guided him back the way she'd come from.

"Yeah," he said, "Turd is an awful name for a dog."

She chuckled. "I think so too. Oh, baby, it's so good to see you. I was so scared…"

***

When they got back to the camp, Dad was alone. Jude ran to him, hugged him hard. So hard, his father nearly toppled over backward. Dad grunted and Jude stopped squeezing so hard. Then his dad thumped him on the back twice. His thumps, usually strong and hard, felt like a bird's wing against Jude's spine. Jude was glad Dad was awake again.

"Where's Tim?" Mom asked, making room on the ground near Jude's dad for him to sit next to his father. Scout circled the family and then trotted around the campsite, sniffing the ground and low-hanging bushes.

"He's looking around," Dad said. "Looking for signs of the bats. He's obsessed with them."

Jude nodded. "Yeah. He got excited when I told him that we'd seen a colony. I—I didn't tell him about the giant bats,

169

but he guessed it."

"He already knew about them," Dad said. "Sounds like he's been researching them and their whereabouts for years."

"Really?" Mom asked. She'd leaned back against a nearby tree and was using a shirt sleeve to wipe her face clean. Her hand moved in slow, tired circles. She caught Jude's eye and smiled.

"Craziest thing," Dad said. He shifted on the pallet of clothes and winced when he moved his leg. "They only migrate here every ten years or so, that's what he said. He's been chasing them in other states—New England and once out west when there were supposed sightings—sounds pretty desperate to find them."

"Why?" Mom asked.

"He wants to get one of them alive. Thinks he'll make a lot of money, selling it to the government or science and research groups. He thinks there is something special about its growth pattern. That it started out as a regular bat and because of a genetic mutation or change in environment, it's morphed into this super bat. Freak bat is more like it," Dad said and grunted as he shifted on the ground.

"When are they coming to rescue us?" Jude asked. "I can't wait to get home."

"Me either," Mom said. "And get your father to a hospital."

Dad just closed his eyes for a minute. When he opened them again, Jude noticed how red they were.

"Tim hasn't given me the radio yet. He said he had a few more questions for you," he looked at Mom, "and that as soon as those were answered he'd let us call for help."

Mom swore under her breath, then glanced guiltily at Jude. "Sorry," she said. "But what else does he need to know? You told him where to go, right?"

Dad nodded.

"Then how can I help him?" Her voice was frustrated and louder than before.

"I don't know," Dad said. He closed his eyes again and this time didn't reopen them. "I'm just going to rest a couple of minutes. He said he was just making a loop and would be back soon."

Jude felt his happiness leak out just a little. He was glad to be back with his family, happy that they were okay. But he wanted to get out of here. Wanted to go home. And stupid Tim and his dumb bats were keeping Jude and his parents stuck here.

"Why can't we just get the radio from him? There are three of us and only one of him," he said.

"It's not a good idea, buddy," Dad said, his eyes still closed. His voice sounded sleepy and slow. "I'm not exactly at my strongest and you and your mom are exhausted and beat up too. Plus, he's got a pack with God knows what sort of weapons in it, not to mention that dog—"

"Scout wouldn't hurt us!"

Dad smiled faintly with his eyes still shut. "Scout?"

"Yeah. He's a good dog. And he's really smart. He stayed with me during the night when I was cold…"

"Tim's coming back," Mom said and Dad's eyes fluttered open.

Sure enough, Jude saw the older man's lanky frame slip from the right side of the cavern, poke his head in, look around the ground, and then walk out toward Jude and his parents.

Dad struggled to sit upright. He'd half-slid down onto his good side.

"Help me, buddy," he said and Jude pulled him into a sitting position. The dirty bandage covering Dad's leg looked soggy and smelled bad.

"Well, you made it back safe," Tim said without smiling. He nodded to Mom and Jude. "Told you that dog's a good tracker."

"Yes. He is," Mom said. "I'd like the radio please." She stood up. Her arms were scraped and bruised, her neck and face were too. But she'd washed away most of the dirt and her eyes when she looked at Tim, were clear and hard. Jude knew that look. Mom was pissed.

Tim looked from Mom to the cavern and back again.

"You know, a real man would help get my husband out of the woods," Mom's voice was so quiet Jude could hardly hear it. "You can see he's in no state to hike out of here." Mom waved toward Dad.

Tim swallowed once, hard, and shook his head. "Sorry," he muttered. "Can't do that." He fumbled in his pack though and handed Mom a small, old-looking radio. "It won't work here," he jerked his head back toward the cavern. "Something about the magnetic field in the rocks. But a short hike back towards Osmore Pond and you'll get a signal."

Mom took the radio but didn't say anything, just stared hard at Tim.

"All I ask is that you leave. Quickly."

"Well, how—"

"I don't know," the words were loud and sharp, like a whip cracking. Tim rubbed a hand over his forehead and paced a few feet away. "Look, lady, I'm trying to help you. It's not safe here. It's time to leave."

Mom glared at Tim for a few seconds then nodded once. "Fine."

"You won't be able to use the radio till you're near the river," Tim said. He motioned to Rick. "Get him to the hospital as soon as you can."

Mom rolled her eyes and clipped the radio onto the waistband of her shorts. "Thanks. I never would have thought of that on my own."

Tim grunted and snapped for the dog. A hot ache spread through Jude's chest as he realized he wouldn't see Scout again.

"Mom," he started, but she was busy helping Dad get to his feet.

"Come on, baby," Mom said to him. "We've got to hurry. Dad needs our help."

"Good luck," Tim called to them, and then he and Scout walked away. Jude felt a ball of tears in his throat and tried to swallow them down.

Scout looked over his shoulder once, whined and wagged his tail, then turned and followed Tim.

Chapter 26

Vernon Heath

"And you're sure this is the right place?" Geoffrey asked again.

"I said I was, didn't I?" Vernon's voice was hard and rough.

"Let's just make sure we know what we're doing," Tess said, her voice gentle. "Vernon, you know the passage to read?"

Vernon didn't bother to answer other than to nod. He'd be glad when this was all over. One way or the other he hoped he wouldn't have to see Geoffrey or Tess or any of the others again. Either the mission would be a success and the bats would be dead, or he would be. He hoped for the former but had accepted the latter a long time ago. Without Mary—

"This has to be it," Tess said, already climbing up toward the hole high in the tunnel's wall. The opening was just as the woman, Marion, had described it.

"I'm not sure that it is—" Geoffrey's voice had a whiney edge that sawed at the edges of Vernon's nerves.

"Come on, Sally," Vernon said. "It's the right place. If you're backing out, that's one thing."

The other man made a disgusted noise in his throat but

shook his head.

"Then let's get in there before they leave," Vernon said.

"Fine. And for the record, I would appreciate it if you wouldn't call me that," Geoffrey replied.

Vernon just smirked and hustled in front of Tess. The woman at least was practical and down-to-earth. He'd met her—what? Four? Five years ago? She'd found out about the group through the friend of a friend and started coming regularly. She'd moved back to Vermont after retiring from the park service in Maine. Wanted to be closer to her family. But then her family had gotten pissed—maybe more so because she was so normal in her regular life. So undramatic. Then they got hit with this: giant, man-eating bats. An ancient curse from a Vermont witch. Now one of Tess's son's only let her spend time with his kids when he or his wife were there to supervise. "He thinks I'm crazy," she'd admitted one night at a meeting. "Doesn't trust me around my own grandkids." Others in the group hadn't fared much better when they'd shared their beliefs. Most of them learned to keep their lips shut and thoughts to themselves. Those that had tried to explain the situation had gotten similar responses as Tess. Either their kids laughed in their faces or started to ask them lots of questions that Vernon imagined you'd hear in a quack's office. "And do you hear voices, Mom?" Or "Where's the proof that all of this is true?" Vernon was less impressed with Geoffrey. Pansy ass. One of those men who threw money at problems and never got his hands dirty. Vernon had only agreed to let him come at Tess's insistence over eight months of reasoning.

Vernon turned his head and spat. It wasn't for a family that he was doing this. Not anymore. He and Mary had never had kids, despite years of trying. No, Vernon was doing this only for Mary. Or at least, her memory. That was all he had now. Even the dog was gone. For the first time in Vernon's sixty-plus years, he was alone.

An image of the dog came to him suddenly. Vernon had sent him away, back to the boy, when he'd arrived at the tunnel's entrance. This was no place for a dog. He'd just get in the way or make noise.

"No," Vernon had said.   Turd had whined in response, thumped his tail a couple of times.

"Go!" Vernon motioned toward the little family which had been barely visible. "Get outta here."

The dog had cocked his head, then turned and retraced his steps. He'd stopped every few feet and looked back as though asking, "Is this really what you mean?"

"Get outta here," Vernon had repeated and turned away. He'd told himself the lump in his throat was due to thirst.

He cleared his throat now, the sound loud in the quiet tunnel. Geoffrey had stopped his sniveling and Tess was quiet behind Vernon as the trio pulled themselves up toward the opening in the tunnel wall.

If this was the spot, then it would soon all be over. Everything Vernon and the others had been working toward all these years—it would finally end. He wanted to feel around in his bag again, feel the small, hard outline of the little book. But there wasn't time or space now to stop again.

Vernon pulled himself up closer to the hole in the wall. When he was at eye level, he cast his flashlight around the space. Below him was a steep descent. To the sides, the rock-studded walls were covered in stones of all different sizes and shapes. Above, he could barely make out the ceiling, dark and mottled. He motioned to the others to wait, then pulled himself through the opening. It took longer than he thought and for a second, he wasn't sure he and his bag would make it. But his frame was hard and sinewy from all the hours spent in the woods and finally, his legs, then his pelvis and torso slid through.

He got his footing before sticking a hand through to help Tess but she handed him her pack instead.

"It's going to be tight," she said. Then, "Can you give me some room?"

Vernon nodded, then realized that she couldn't see him and mumbled yes, before climbing over a pile of stones and positioning himself to the right of the opening.

He thought about how it had all started. Vernon had been one of the group's earliest members, but not the first. That had been Nathan Carvell. Some big-name genealogist—Vernon hadn't even known there was such a thing—Nathan tracked down people's families for a living. It had started with one strange book—a copy of which Vernon now held in his hand—a journal that Nathan had discovered in an unusual bookshop in a tiny town in southwestern Vermont. Place wasn't open anymore, the owners had gone bankrupt. The journal though had been written by a woman named Sarah Ann Krupp. She'd been a recluse and a witch.

The tiny journal had sparked a fire in Nathan. He'd become obsessed, digging into old records and books until he'd finally found what he was looking for: a Vermont folklore book that spoke of the curse of Vermont's best-known witch. While the story of the Salem witch trials was remembered well, a witch trial held in southern Vermont was not. Didn't mean it didn't happen, Vernon thought as he swerved around a large stone in the path and warned Tess to do the same.

Sarah Ann had lived in a small town in the southern part of the state. She'd led a quiet life, according to her journal, but there had been frequent run-ins with religious authorities. Strange happenings around her property, people she disliked getting sick. As in any small town, talk festered and Sarah Ann was formally accused of being a witch. The townspeople had eventually seen her hang off the edge of a bridge.

"Need help?" Vernon asked Tess softly. She was climbing through the opening but it was a tight squeeze, as she'd predicted. Her shoulders and hips were both wider than his.

"No," she said, panting. "Just give me another minute."

Vernon thought again about the little journal tucked into his bag. Along with the woman's references to things that grew in her garden, it contained a Record of Deeds. These were things Sarah Ann had witnessed and punished or those that other townspeople had brought to her under the cover of darkness.

Like any typical small town, many were silly: "Mrs. Benjamin stole Mrs. Peabody's family apple pie recipe," and the like. Others were more sinister. "Mr. Jakes beat Mr. Marlin within an inch of his life after the latter was seen walking his younger daughter home from the parade."

There were spells too, most of which Vernon and the others in the group couldn't decipher. Most importantly though, on the last page of the journal was a curse that Sarah Ann had written while on house arrest. She'd remained in her own home at the end, barricaded and awaiting death. The curse was written—and given one had to imagine—to her accusers. Below those two paragraphs, was another with a simple heading: "For Reversal". Why she'd included it, Vernon couldn't imagine. What possible motive would she have?

Maybe in the end her anger had turned to fear or she was more frightened of her dark deeds than of the hatred she must have felt for those in the town who'd turned on her. Or at least, not raised a hand in her defense.

The more Nathan had learned in his research, the more impassioned he'd become. He had searched for decades to tease more information about the woman out of historical records from around the state. What had started as simple curiosity became much more. Particularly when Nathan learned an extremely startling fact: his family line descended from one of Sarah Ann's accusers.

Tess grunted and dropped through the hole, slipping before she gained her footing. Breathing hard she nodded when Vernon asked if she was all right, then moved off to the left to free up room for Geoffrey to get down.

Vernon's thoughts turned back to Nathan and this foolhardy attempt to set things right. Vernon wasn't too technical but apparently, Nathan had put more of the pieces together over time. He'd found other descendants of the townspeople who'd murdered Sarah Ann. Vernon couldn't even imagine approaching these other New Englanders with the story. He shook his head thinking about it. He'd had gumption, Nathan had. No one could say he didn't.

Most of the families had dismissed Nathan. Even after he showed them the journal, half laughed in his face while the other half had guided him to the door with looks of pity on their faces, he'd recounted in a meeting.

"Does anyone have an extra light?" Geoffrey asked, his voice interrupting Vernon's thoughts. His head stuck through the opening.

"Where's yours?" Tess asked in a whisper.

"The batteries just died."

Tess shook her head. "Sorry. You can share mine."

Vernon squinted at the man and shook his head. Geoffrey was a professor, and both of his kids were some big-wig types, lawyers or doctors, or something.

"I feel like I'm leading a double life," Geoffrey had said once at a meeting, while the group sipped burned coffee out of Styrofoam cups. "I live in fear that they'll find out. And of what will happen if they don't. If they are attacked."

Stupid as the man was, he was right to worry, Vernon had thought. There had been three instances since he'd started attending the group nearly seven years ago. The curse had been written specifically for the descendants of the townspeople. Those who had put Sarah Ann on trial. As far as anyone in the group could tell, there was no time limit, no expiration date for it.

Three different people had come forward with horror stories, two happening to members of the group. The third joined after learning about it from a friend of a friend. The first "accident" had happened on a desolate road. A car carrying one of the member's kids had plunged down an embankment. It had been dusk and the road dry. There had been a lot of blood and a broken windshield. Wild animals were accused of dismembering the body before it was found, but the mother, Debbie, had sworn it was the bats.

Another two members had lost their children or grandkids in similar ways. But there too, the roads or hiking paths were desolate and there had been too much damage to the bodies to verify the cause of death in any of the cases. One was considered a freak auto accident, the second death attributed to a fall while hiking.

The only similarities between the accidents were that they always happened in the same type of place: remote forests and woods. Places where giant bats could live unfettered and unharmed for years, generations even. Not that they lived here year-round. These bats migrated, flying south to desolate areas in New Mexico and Arizona, Vernon had heard from other members, before returning north every few years. There didn't seem to be much rhyme or reason to the migration pattern. Unlike other animals, the bats didn't travel annually or even to the same locations every time. It had made tracking them hard. Anticipating their next moves was like a crapshoot and Vernon himself wasn't much of a gambler.

Geoffrey dropped through the opening in the rocks, his head barely clearing the stone.

He let out a shaky laugh and held on tight to the side of the wall. "It's steep, isn't it?"

Vernon didn't bother to respond to such a stupid observation.

"Just so we're on the same page," Geoffrey continued, "the plan is still the same, right?"

"Right," Tess said, her voice just low enough for the men to hear. "I can see some there," she pointed toward the ceiling, the flashlight's beam just outlining what looked like water stains. Vernon squinted. The stains moved as one, readjusting their position on the ceiling.

"We'll have to get down to the floor and place the candles." Tess motioned with the light below them. "We'll recite the reversal text there. And then, when the bats fly, we kill them." Her voice was matter of fact, as though she was recounting a recipe for apple pie or the most outrageous headline in the day's paper. "Only the giant ones though, not the others. With

181

the curse lifted, there won't be a problem with those."

"Let's hope," Geoffrey said. "I've been practicing my aim with the bolas but am still not as accurate as I'd like."

Tess made an appreciative noise but Vernon ignored him. Bolas were made with three lengths of rope, tied together at one end. This was held in the hand. The other ends were each tied securely around stones of equal size. Whirling it around one's head, the bola was then released, knocking into and killing one's prey. Or even better, strangling it at the same time the stones slammed viciously into its skull.

The decision to use only primitive weapons to kill the bats had been argued. Some in the group thought the fashioning of the weapons and training with them would be next to impossible. Others sided with Nathan who believed that other types of weapons would not be successful against the bats. The Reversal clearly stated, "I kill ye by my hand" and he believed that a gun or explosives would not be effective.

In the end, the group had voted: only primitive weapons could be used, and only those which the member had made by hand. The knife that Vernon brought with him wasn't officially allowed. But Tess and Geoffrey didn't need to know he'd brought it.

"Do you see any of the big ones?" Geoffrey asked and craned his neck. For no particular reason, Vernon wanted to punch the other man squarely in his weaselly, sweating face. Instead, he shook his head. The trio was silent for a few minutes. A trickle of sweat meandered down Vernon's back.

"There," he said softly seconds later. He pointed his light beam toward the ceiling to the far right of where their little group huddled. "There."

Geoffrey and Tess were silent a moment, then Tess made a

little gasping sound.

At that moment the bat's head swiveled toward them.

And opened its eyes.

Chapter 27

Rick Langlois

"Stop, please," Rick's voice little more than a whisper. What was happening to him? He'd been getting better, but now...not anymore. His leg and entire side burned. Felt like his clothes had been ignited in flames. Sweat beaded on his forehead and ran down the back of his neck. His mouth was pasty. A bad smell came from between his lips. Worst of all, he could barely walk. He stumbled every couple of steps, leaning more and more heavily on Marion and Jude.

"Here, let's rest on this log," Marion's voice was close to his ear. It sounded like a trumpet. He jerked back. The three of them nearly toppled to the ground. Jude yelped and grabbed for Rick's side. His fingers grabbed at the deep gouges there.

Rick grit his teeth. The moan came out anyway.

"Sorry. Sorry, Dad," Jude said and moved his hand. They helped Rick lean against a downed tree. He heard his breath, rattling, and gasping. Knew that it should scare him, how bad it sounded, but was too tired to care.

"Leave me," he wanted to tell his family. Again. But already knew what Marion would say.

"Can you drink this?" she asked. Rick felt the ribbed mouth

of the water bottle pressed against his lips.

He gulped at it greedily, choked a little, and then drank some more. The bottle disappeared when he was done. Neat trick, he thought. The trees around him swirled and twisted like they were dancing to some music he couldn't hear. The sight made his stomach turn. He closed his eyes. Groaned again.

"Please go," he mumbled. "Please leave me."

"We're not leaving anyone," Marion said, her voice unnaturally cheerful. "We'll be out of here before you know it."

"Mom, can I try the radio?"

Rick heard nylon rustle. Marion must be doing something in the pack. Did she have medicine? But no, he remembered that she'd said she had already given him the last of it.

"Tim said it wouldn't work out here."

"But can't I just try it?"

"We should save the battery."

Jude sighed heavily and the dog gave a little whine. What was the dog's name again? Rick thought hard. Something stupid. Bathroom related. He was glad that Jude had the dog even if it did have a stupid name. The kid had wanted a pet for ages, but Marion hadn't been thrilled with the idea.

"Please, Mom? It wouldn't hurt to just try."

More rustling in the pack. "What?" Marion's voice was distracted with a frustrated edge. Then, "Fine. Sure, go ahead."

"Okay. What should I say?"

"What? Oh, I don't know. Mayday, mayday? Help us we're lost in the forest?" Marion's voice was bitter now, angry-sounding. Did she blame Rick? She should.

"Uh…hello? Mayday, mayday. This is the Langlois family. We're lost in the forest in Groton. Please, can anyone hear me?"

185

No sound, other than the continued sound of nylon rubbing together. "Where is that stupid thing?" Marion mumbled, then sighed.

"Mom? Do you think anyone heard me?"

"I don't know, baby. Why don't you try again?"

A fly—a loud one—was buzzing around Rick's head. He wanted to swat it away. Too tired. It landed on his cheek.

"This is the Langlois family—Jude, Marion, and Rick Langlois. We were camping at Groton State Forest but are lost in the woods. My dad is hurt. Please, can anyone hear me?"

There was no reply.

Finally, the nylon sound stopped. "Better turn it off, Jude. Save the battery for when we can get a good signal."

"Let me leave it on just a few more minutes. I mean, someone might have heard but they can't get to the radio right now. Maybe they're in the bathroom. Just a couple more minutes, okay?"

"Fine. But I wouldn't get my hopes up. We don't even know if we're on a good channel. We could be—"

"Roger that, Langlois family. This is Ben Wilcox. What's your 2-20?"

Marion gasped.

"Mom! Mom, did you hear that?" Jude's voice was incredulous.

"Yes, yes! Answer him. Tell him we don't know but we're somewhere northeast of the lake."

"We don't know where we are. Somewhere northeast of the lake. We got lost. Can you help us? My dad's hurt real bad. And we don't have any food left. And my—"

"Jude, let him answer." Marion's voice cut in.

"Okay."

Silence for a second. A bird tweeted loudly overhead.

"Roger that, who am I speaking to?"

"Mom!"

Some rustling and then the click of a button.

"Yes, this is Marion. Marion Langlois. My family and I got lost out here in the woods. We're so glad to hear your voice."

Marion was crying, Rick thought. He wanted to comfort her. Tell her everything would be all right. But he couldn't move. Even breathing had become hard.

"All right, ma'am. I'm near the ranger station. Let me get him to call you back, all right?"

"Okay," Marion said. "Thank you."

"You just hold tight, ma'am."

The silence after the voice faded was huge.

"Mom, did you hear that?" Jude asked. "He's going to get the ranger to call us! We'll be out of here before long, right?"

"Right," Marion said. Rick heard fear laced in her voice.

"How long before the ranger calls us?"

"I'm not sure. Jude, can you take the dog over there for a few minutes? I need to check your dad's bandage."

"It's all right, I don't mind seeing it."

"No. It's best if I do this alone."

"Okay. Should I take the radio with me?"

"Sure. Just run back if the ranger calls you, okay? I want to hear what he says too."

"Okay," Jude's voice faded. Rick heard the sound of feet moving over dry leaves.

"Honey?" Marion's voice was close to his face. Why was she so loud? He wanted to put his hands up to muffle the sound.

Maybe he'd winced because she was quieter when she spoke again. "I found the last of the clean bandages. I need to change

187

the dressing. Your fever's back and whatever you used to bring it down isn't working anymore."

Rick tried to respond but all that came out was a groan.

"This might be a little uncomfortable. I'll go as quickly as I can though."

He didn't bother trying to respond. He heard rustling as she pulled something out of the bag. That was what she had been looking for. Clean bandages. I wonder if I'll feel this? Rick thought dreamily. Then an electricity bolt of pain when she pulled away the bandages.

Everything started to fade. The light above, the sounds of the forest. He could hear Marion's breathing though, and her voice whispering as she talked to herself. He focused on that. What was she saying? Was she talking to him? He couldn't make out the sentences, just words: "help me," and "oh my God," and then the sound of something like she was choking. No, not exactly choking. Crying?

Feet moving nearby through leaves. It sounded muted like it was underwater.

"Mom! Mom, I have the park ranger on the phone. I mean the radio—oh!" Jude's voice turned into a retch.

"Jude!"

More rustling. Fire licked at Rick's leg and side. He couldn't smell the smoke but the flames were incredibly hot.

"Hello?" Marion's voice whispered from somewhere far away. "Hello? This is Marion Langlois. My family and I—"

And then everything went dark.

Chapter 28

Vernon Heath

"Shut the lights off," Vernon hissed, flicking the switch on his flashlight. Tess fumbled with hers a second before he heard the click. The sound was loud in the quiet cavern, where every noise echoed. Vernon held his breath. He half expected to feel the giant bat above him, grabbing at his head, his shoulders. But after a few long minutes, nothing had happened.

"We'll have to get down to the bottom with the lights muted," he said.

"How?" Tess asked.

"Put your hand or some piece of your clothes over it. Filter it so it's not so bright."

"I don't understand," Geoffrey spoke up. Too loud. He was too loud for the quiet space. "Aren't they blind?"

"I don't know," Vernon whispered, "and keep your voice down. Anyway, I don't want to take any chances. Do you? It looked right in our direction; didn't you see it?"

"Yes," Geoffrey's voice was quiet.

"Let's go," Vernon said.

Making their way down the steep, rock-filled ravine was

189

hard. Vernon was best equipped for it, spending most of his time outdoors and in the woods and mountains. But even his arms shook when they were only halfway down. Around him, he listened for noises of the bats moving. He could hear a very high-pitched sound coming from above and the occasional scrabbling of claws on stone as the bats rearranged their positions slightly on the stone ceiling.

Behind him, Geoffrey stumbled, lost his footing. His leg shot out and nearly clipped Vernon in the side.

"Hey," he muttered quietly. "Watch it."

"I'm sorry but I can't see a thing," Geoffrey complained in a loud whisper.

"We're nearly there now," Tess said, encouragingly. She couldn't see much either if she thought that, Vernon mused.

It seemed to take a month to reach the cavern's floor. Finally, though, they all stood on level ground again. Vernon motioned the other two close and then whispered to them.

"We'll get to that wide, flat rock. Put the candles up there. And then Tess can start the reading."

Geoffrey let out a strangled-sounding cough and Vernon elbowed him in the ribs, hard.

"Hey, what—" Geoffrey's whine was again too loud. Vernon felt his hand ball into a fist.

"Come on, boys," Tess whispered. "Let's get this over with so we can get out of here and get back home."

Home. The word sounded foreign to Vernon. Without Mary where was home? Their house was an empty box now, lifeless. He remembered a little wooden plaque Mary had kept in the kitchen, hanging over the sink. "Home is where your heart is". It was true. And that meant that Vernon's heart was six feet under. He readjusted his pack on his shoulder, closed his mind to the thoughts. Nothing good ever came of them.

Slowly, Vernon walked toward the long, flat stone. It was smeared with something black and oozy looking—bat shit most likely—and he avoided those areas as he laid out the candles. Next, he pulled out the little journal. It felt warm and dry in his hands. He closed his eyes a second, thought of the others in their little group. If they were successful today, how much would their lives change?

And if they weren't?

"Here, take these," he shoved a small box of waterproof matches into Tess's hand. "And you," he turned to Geoffrey and handed him the knife. "Take this and don't you dare drop it."

Geoffrey grunted something unintelligible.

Vernon brought the little book close to his face. He'd memorized the words. Had lots of time these days. Even so, he wanted the text there, to remind him if he forgot.

The first match hissed and Vernon held his breath. No sound from above but he didn't dare to shine the light up there again. Tess held the match's tip to the first candle. After a few seconds, she tipped it sideways, letting some of the wax pool on the large stone, and then set the candle in it. It held fast.

She moved to the second one then the third and fourth. By the time she'd gotten to the sixth, Vernon had opened the little journal to the right page. He closed his eyes briefly, took a deep breath, and began.

Convertere, ut maledicat: Oro te, ne ultra sanguis ejus sit super me manus. Non peto ut amor sit, sed quia spiritu suo in pace.

The words, in Latin, fell in clumps from Vernon's mouth. He'd

191

looked up each in a little dictionary at home, knew both the English and Latin words by heart. But still, they felt stiff and awkward on his tongue.

Reverse this curse, I pray thee, that no more blood shall be on my hands. It is not for love I ask it, but for my own spirit's peace.

Vernon repeated the phrase in Latin, then a third time. The words came more easily now, the sentences growing louder to be heard over the noise—wait, what was that noise? Vernon opened his eyes. The light from the white candles flickered and spit in the humidity of the cavern. Vernon chanced it. Poked the light of his flashlight overhead. The bats shifted on the ceiling high above. Their bodies rolled in waves, first in one direction and then another. The sound was their wings moving against one and other, Vernon realized. It sounded like a hundred newspaper pages turning at once.

"What's happening?" Geoffrey asked in a hoarse whisper.

"Shh," Tess said. "Look!" She jabbed a finger toward the spot where the biggest bat had hung. It was unfurling its wings. Was it about to take flight? Vernon spoke the phrase again in English and then once more in Latin. Tess's voice joined in and then Geoffrey's. They had to say it louder as the sounds above grew. Hissing filled the air then, like a thousand snakes slithering on the high ceiling.

Geoffrey gasped, pulled Vernon to the ground, and Tess with his other hand. The giant bat launched itself from the cavern ceiling and dove toward them and the ring of candles. It screeched, so loudly that Vernon clapped both hands over his ears instinctively, muffled the sound of the piercing cry. Then there was a pulse of some sort of energy—it was like an electric bolt, Vernon thought—but without the pain. It numbed his hands and arms. He'd dropped the book and fumbled to pick it up again.

The page. Where was the page he'd been reading from? He tried to bring them to mind but his head felt full of wool. He flipped through the little journal, his fingers slow and his brain moving at half speed…

"Look out!" Tess yelled. Geoffrey scrabbled around on the ground.

"I can't find the knife!" he shouted. The big bat dropped toward them. Seconds away. Its wingspan was huge, its body the size of a medium-sized dog. It drew closer. Then closer still. Maybe feet away now?

Vernon found the page. He yelled the words aloud at the same time wondering: was this the one? Was this bat the last thing his Mary had seen before she'd died?

Convertere, ut maledicat: Oro te, ne ultra sanguis ejus sit super me manus. Non peto ut amor sit, sed quia spiritu suo in pace.

He screamed the words now. The bat veered crookedly to the right. Its face was gray and wizened looking, like a pug crossed with a monkey. Its mouth was open. A row of serrated teeth—white against the dark fur—shone out. Geoffrey squealed. Tess brandished a throwing star she'd made from green tree branches, the tips razor sharp. But before she'd had a chance to throw it the creature swung out of range. It hissed and screeched and then careened into a nearby boulder.

Vernon heard loud crunching sounds as the bat's body collided with the immovable stone surface. A dark liquid stained the rock and the bat slid down, then fell heavily to the stones below. They'd done it. The curse had been broken.

"It's working!" Tess yelled. "It's working, Vernon!"

Vernon turned to look at her. Behind her was something that shouldn't be there. His mind still stupidly slow, Vernon watched puzzled as Tess sprouted a pair of dark wings.

"Tess, look out!"

It was behind her. Another one, bigger than the first. Tess looked at him, mouth opened in surprise but no sound came out. The bat's dark talons sunk into her collarbone. Then she screamed, her face anguished. It lifted her off the ground, its wings *whap-whap-whapping* at the air like a helicopter blade.

"No!" Vernon looked for the knife. It was still in Geoffrey's hand which was frozen in mid-air. He grabbed it, shoved the other man out of the way. But the bat had flown too high for Vernon to reach.

"Get the bolas!" he yelled and Geoffrey, moving in slow motion took off his pack.

Vernon couldn't see Tess anymore, but Mary. Mary's body being lifted off the ground. Mary being taken—oh God. It was happening again.

"No," Vernon shouted a second time and half ran, half tripped after the bat. Tess screamed. The sound was horrible, tortured, and panicked.

Geoffrey was moaning, "Oh, no, oh no," over and over again as he fumbled in the pack.

"Hurry up!" Vernon whirled, shoved the man with his shoulder. "Stop cowering and help me!"

Geoffrey stood, looking dazed. "I can't—I don't know where they are. They must have slipped down when we were—"

Vernon didn't wait to hear the rest. He couldn't see the bat anymore but went in the direction it had flown. He heard the loud hissing overhead, but the smaller bats still clung to the ceiling.

He'd been so stupid. The incantation hadn't worked. They'd all die in here.

Vernon lunged over a big stone. He caught a glimpse of something from the corner of his eye and shone the light in that direction.

The bat circled erratically. Tess hung limply in its grasp. Was she—Vernon scrambled over another boulder.

The bat flew back toward a large stone where Geoffrey and Vernon had been just seconds before. It dropped Tess. Her body arched through the air, her clothes made a little rippling sound before she landed, hard. If she hadn't been unconscious before, she was now.

The creature flew over Tess's body, made two tight circles, and landed. It stood over her like a hawk with its prey, wings spread out, blocking Vernon's view. He ran toward it, his progress too slow. Rocks and stones tripped him, made it difficult to get his footing.

The bat threw its head back and made the same horrible sound—half screech, half guttural choke—and the bats on the ceiling above started to move. Vernon stopped. He stared upward. The wave began again. The smaller bats lifted off the ceiling like a curtain and dove toward the big bat. It gave another crowing shriek. The bats moved in a formation and as one, dove toward Tess's prone figure.

"No!" Vernon yelled. But he didn't run forward. He could see from here that he was too late. Geoffrey's pale face peeked out from behind a stone a few yards beyond the stone ledge. It looked like a moon, white and wide. He too, stared in horror as the bats fed.

He'd killed Tess by bringing her here. Just like Mary.

Vernon closed his eyes, swayed on his feet.

It had been an unseasonably warm September night. They'd gone camping, just a short weekend getaway before Mary had started work again at the nursing home. She'd lost her mother only a few weeks before and had taken time off to grieve and sort through the house.

It had been beautiful that night: the moon had been full, the light so bright that Mary had teased they'd never get to sleep. They'd laid out under the stars like they used to when they'd first been married. And Mary had pointed out constellations to him until his eyes had closed. He'd fallen asleep to the sound of her voice and the feeling of a soft summer-like breeze on his face.

He'd woken to her screams. The bat had taken her, sleeping bag and all. Vernon had watched, blinking, unable to grasp what he was seeing. *I'm dreaming, I must be dreaming,* he'd thought. Then he'd seen the bat readjust its hold and the sleeping bag had fallen…such a long way down. And Vernon had grabbed for his backpack and his gun. He'd aimed, finger feathered on the trigger but the bat had been too close to Mary. He never could have hit it without getting her.

In the end, it hadn't mattered.

They'd found the body three days later. Funny how a person goes from having a name to being referred to as an "it", Vernon had thought when the medical examiner explained that there wasn't much left of his wife to identify.

And now it had happened again.

Chapter 29

Jude Langlois

"Baby, why don't you let me call Mrs. Baker. You can stay at her house until things calm down."

Jude shook his head stubbornly. His mother had been trying to get him to go to the neighbor's house since they'd arrived at the hospital. But he wasn't going. Dad was still in ICU. Jude didn't know what that stood for but the grownups talked about it like it was a big deal so he guessed it was where the sickest people went. And even though the chairs in the waiting room were hard, they were closer to where Dad was.

"Will you come?" Jude asked Mom.

She shook her head. Her back was covered in bandages that peeked up over the collar of a clean T-shirt someone had given her. It was too big and she looked kind of funny especially since she still wore her dirty pants and muddy boots. From the top up she looked clean even though she was covered in scratches, but the rest of her looked like she'd been through a zombie apocalypse.

"I can't," she said softly. "But you—"

"I'm staying too," Jude said and ran a hand over Scout's neck.

197

The dog gave two tail thumps in response. Dogs weren't allowed in the hospital, the nurse had told his mother but after hearing their tale she'd said they'd be able to make an exception, just this once. She'd put them in a little room off of the waiting area where no one would see Scout and Jude had promised to keep him quiet.

Mom sighed and ran a hand over Jude's hair. It was still dirty. She'd been picking pieces of bark and twigs and leaves out of it while they'd been waiting.

"All right," she said. Then patted his knee twice and stood up. "I'm going to go and talk to the doctor. Would you like something else from the vending machine?"

Jude shook his head. His stomach was stuffed with all the junk food his mother never usually let him have. He felt a little sick but didn't tell her.

"No, I'm good."

"Okay, I'll be back soon."

Jude nodded. He yawned and rested his head back in his chair. He'd slept off and on since the rescue team had delivered them to the hospital. It was two towns over, in St. Johnsbury. Jude had never been so glad to see a sink or toilet or vending machine in his life.

There was a light knock on the open door.

"Hey, it's Jude right?" a voice asked. Jude's eyelids snapped open. The game warden, Mr. Matthews, stood above him. Jude straightened up.

"Mind if I sit down?" Mr. Matthews asked, and waved a big hand toward the nearby chair.

Jude shook his head. Scout whined and Jude patted the dog's shoulder. "It's okay, boy."

"Good looking dog you've got there," the warden said. His

dark skin reminded Jude of hot chocolate. Mmm, cocoa sounded good right now. As though reading his mind, Mr. Matthews motioned to the hallway.

"Would you like to walk down and get a cup of something hot? Coffee or latte? Oh, uh, I guess your mom wouldn't like that. They have cocoa in the machine too."

Jude nodded. "Sure," he said. "If Scout can come."

Mr. Matthews smiled broadly. "Absolutely."

The three walked down the hall. Jude's legs still felt rubbery. Mr. Matthews pointed out some old photos on the wall as they walked. They were really old black and white pictures where fuzzy faces stared at the camera. It looked like everyone was mad. Jude told Mr. Matthews that and he chuckled.

"Well, those were different times. People had to work hard back then and there wasn't a lot of fun in their lives I guess."

"Yeah, we learned about the Colonial times and Westward Expansion in history," Jude offered. "Kids didn't get to play much back then."

"No," Mr. Matthews agreed and shook his head. "Here we are," he stopped in front of a machine that had a sign that flashed "Hot Coffee!" and had a bunch of different buttons on the side.

"One cocoa and one extra-dark coffee coming up." Mr. Matthews fed some dollar bills into the machine. "Oh, and one dog biscuit for your friend," he said and handed Jude a small, old-looking bone-shaped treat from his pocket. "I keep them handy for campers' dogs. Makes them friendlier," he said.

Jude smiled and gave the biscuit to Scout who crunched it twice before swallowing it down. He looked back at the warden, wagged his tail. Mr. Matthews laughed.

"Sorry, buddy, that's all I've got with me," he said.

"So, Jude," the game warden asked after they'd collected their drinks and were walking back to the little room. "Can you tell me more about his man who helped you in the woods? Tim, you said, right?"

Jude nodded. He liked how the man listened closely to what you were saying. Mr. Matthews had done the same thing when he and the other rescuers had first found Jude and his parents. He'd been calm and quiet when Mom had burst into tears and started babbling and had helped to calm her down. Then he'd listened to Jude as they'd hiked back out of the forest. Jude had told him about Tim and Scout and how they'd found him after Jude had almost drowned.

"If I showed you some pictures, could you pick him out do you think?"

Jude nodded. He hoped so. He didn't want to disappoint Mr. Matthews.

"Great," Mr. Matthews said and sighed like he was relieved. "I have them here with me. Let's find a spot for our drinks and you can look through them, okay?"

"Okay," Jude said. Wait till he told Mom and Dad he'd helped the warden! Jude frowned suddenly, thinking about Dad. He didn't like how everyone talked in louder voices when Jude was around. It was almost like two conversations were going on—one between his mother and the nurses and doctors and one with Jude.

"Here we go," Mr. Matthews said as he handed Jude a small brown envelope. Inside, was a stack of glossy pictures. Some of them were like those you see on cop shows on TV where the people looked angry and held onto those white and black things. But others were just regular pictures of people—some of them were in the woods and some were going into and out of a building. Jude strained to see what the name of the building was but couldn't quite make it out.

He turned one picture, then another, looking carefully. He'd made it through most of the stack before he saw him.

"This is him!" he said excitedly. Scout whined and Jude lowered his voice. "This is Tim." He handed the picture to Mr. Matthews.

The big man nodded his head slowly, then looked at Jude with a smile tugging at the corners of his mouth.

"Thanks, Jude. You've been a big help."

"Do you know who he is?" Jude asked, and reached over to take a sip from the paper cup. The cocoa was still too hot and he burned his lips.

"Yes, I know him. And you're right, his name isn't Tim."

"What is it?"

"Vernon. Mr. Vernon Heath."

"Is he…is he bad?"

The warden looked at Jude, studied him for a few seconds, and then shook his head. "Not bad. Just misguided."

Jude didn't know what that meant and didn't ask.

"Is your mom around?"

"Yeah, she just went to talk to the doctor. She should be back soon."

"Good. I'd like to talk to her when she is. Hey listen," Mr. Matthews said and collected the photos, tucked them back into their envelope, and back into his pocket. "Do you think you could draw a map for me? I'm curious where you and your family stayed and how far it was from where we found you."

Jude nodded excitedly. Now he was helping the police—well,

201

a game warden is sort of like a policeman, right?—and probably it would be in the newspaper. He'd show Peyton first, Jude decided, then the rest of his class. Mrs. Pelsky might want to feature it on their "Neighborhood News" bulletin board.

"Yeah, I can do that. I'm good with maps. Well," Jude thought hard. "I'm pretty good with them."

"Great, thanks," Mr. Matthews stood up. "I'll go get some paper and a pen, all right?"

Jude nodded.

"If your mom comes back, can you please let her know I'd like to speak with her?"

"Okay."

The tiredness that had been pulling at Jude had vanished. He took another, bigger swallow of cocoa and let his legs swing underneath the chair. Then he closed his eyes and tried to visualize where they'd been near the cavern to where they'd been when the rescue team had found them. He thought he had a pretty good idea.

When Mr. Matthews came back, Jude carefully drew the picture from his mind. After a few minutes, he sighed.

"I think that's it," he said. Mr. Matthews looked at the map.

"Mind if I take a closer look?" he asked.

Jude shook his head.

Mr. Matthews' eyebrows pulled together as he studied the map. Then he checked something on his phone and pointed to some of the landmarks Jude had drawn.

"What's this big thing here?"

Jude looked. "That's a big cave. That's where we saw the bats."

The warden nodded. "Ah," he said. "And this here?" His finger traced the line to one of the "x's" Jude had drawn halfway between their little camp and where they'd called for help. "Oh, that's a big tree that was down. I marked as many of those as I remembered with 'x's', see?" Jude pointed to two others. "Just the ones that we rested on. The ones that were good for sitting. We had to do that a lot and for a long time too because Dad was hurting."

"I get it," Mr. Matthews said. "This is good, Jude. It will be helpful."

"Are you going to go try to find him?"

"Who? Mr. Heath?"

Jude nodded.

"Yes. I am going to go and try to find him. Mr. Heath is... well. I want to make sure that he's all right out there, in the woods. I'd like him to leave, go back home where he'd be safe, you know?"

Jude frowned and bit his lip. "Mr. Heath went into that cave," he pointed at the drawing. "He was hunting...something."

The warden bent his head a little closer. "Say again?"

"Tim...I mean, Mr. Heath was hunting some bats. But not regular bats. Some giant ones."

"Giant bats," Mr. Matthew repeated.

Jude stole a quick look at him. Mom had told him not to say anything to anyone about the giant bats. She was afraid that they'd think their family was disreputable, whatever that meant. But Jude knew he could trust Mr. Matthews.

"Don't tell my mom I told you," he said, just in case. "She told me that people wouldn't believe us."

Mr. Matthews drew his fingers across his lips as though zipping them shut. "Gotcha," he said and gave Jude a wink.

"Listen, I need to get going," he said. "When your mom comes back, please tell her that I'll be in touch soon, okay?"

Jude nodded. "Okay," he said.

"You take care." Mr. Matthews stood up and gave him a two-finger salute. "Again, good job out there. You're a brave guy."

Scout thumped his tail twice and Jude grinned as he watched the tall game warden walk away. A happy glow spread through Jude's chest. He was almost a hero, really.

Chapter 30

Buzz Matthews

When Byron "Buzz" Matthews pulled out of the parking lot, a familiar tingle ran up his spine. It had been a long time since he'd felt it. He knew the exact time and place he'd felt it last: working as a game warden in Taos. He'd missed it, Buzz thought wryly as he consulted the map once more. Not the heat or the poisonous snakes or the constant pressure to be "on" but the people and the landscape and the excitement that had come with the job.

Meeting Jennifer had changed everything. For the good, he reminded himself. For the most part anyway. But living in New England, in the tiny state of Vermont had been an adjustment. Buzz wasn't used to being stared at. Wasn't used to conversations falling to a hush when he entered a room.

"It's just the uniform," Jennifer had teased him. "And your rugged good looks."

But Buzz knew it was more. Here, he was an outsider, evident by the darkness of his skin. He'd never visited much less lived in a place as white as Vermont. He knew the move had been good for them. When he'd been game warden he'd worked more and more hours as his territory had grown following staff cutbacks. Finally, Jennifer had had enough.

"We never see each other anymore," she'd said, her voice pleading after another tense evening following an emergency phone call. "I don't want to live like this. Like two shadows sharing the same roof but never really being together."

Buzz had been ready to defend himself, to explain again about the nature of his work. But Jennifer knew. Game wardens are the police officers of the woods. Only instead of there being a team of officers working together, it was usually one person per territory that spread many miles. Sometimes hundreds of miles.

"It's not just your job. It's mine, too," Jennifer had said, wrapping her arms around him. "Work has been crazy. I love what I do, but I just—" she'd broken off, her eyes filled with tears. "I just miss you."

And that had started it. Many long hours had followed: planning sessions, ideas tossed around, decisions made. But eventually Jennifer first, then Buzz had quit their jobs. They'd sold their house and made the move north. Jennifer had found a great job at a tech company that allowed her to work part of the week from home. She was originally from upstate New York, so in a way, she was moving back home. But the transition for Buzz hadn't been so smooth.

Vermont was a strange place, he mused not for the first time as he maneuvered the winding roads out of town. The climate was harsh: bitterly cold, snowy winters followed by spring which was affectionately called "mud season". The summers were nice. Cool compared to New Mexico but humid. Then autumn came in all its glory. Buzz liked autumn. What came afterward he didn't enjoy as much.

The people here were...unique. Buzz slowed to pass a

tractor putting along with its green paint shining in the summer's sun. He raised a hand in response to the old farmer who'd waved and given him a nod. New Englanders were known to be reserved, opinionated, and generous if they let you into their circles. The problem was that after four years here, Buzz didn't feel let into any circles. Unless you counted the youth group he and Jennifer were in charge of at their church.

Buzz's cell phone rang and he put it on speaker, focusing on the hairpin turn.

"Matthews," he said.

"It's Craig." A man's booming voice filled the interior of the SUV. "You about here?"

"Craig, good to hear your voice, man. My ETA's for about fifteen minutes."

"Hmm. So you'll be here in thirty?"

Buzz laughed. "Sounds about right."

"Good enough. I'm at the trailhead now. I'll do some bird watching while I wait."

"Thanks, man," Buzz said. "I'll be there shortly."

He disconnected and pressed his foot a little harder on the accelerator. Craig Burns was his closest friend up here. Craig had a background in law enforcement too and had grown up in Vermont. Anxious to get away after school, he'd eventually found himself in Chicago, where he'd worked as a cop for many years. It had left him burned out though, and seeking something completely different. Now he worked as a securities firm investigator—looking into suspected cases of embezzlement, insurance fraud, and other white-collar stuff. He joked that he was the step before calling in the authorities. When businesses—mostly family-owned—wanted to dot their "i's" and cross their "t's" without stepping on toes unnecessarily. Or attracting unwanted press.

Buzz remembered meeting Craig at an outdoor survival training class. Buzz needed it to keep up-to-date with work requirements. Craig was bored and wanted to do something different. They'd hit it off immediately and gotten together in the months following for craft beer tours, mountain biking, and lots and lots of hiking. Craig's current girlfriend and Jennifer knew each other through some work connection—both were in marketing. The four of them often got together on the weekends that Buzz was off, exploring Vermont's outdoor playground.

Buzz slowed for a tight curve and then put his blinker on. He turned off the main road and onto the first of several dirt roads that would lead him to the mountain. His thoughts turned to Vernon Heath and the other people in his little group. Vermont winters were long and Buzz had become familiar with Heath, who lived in the area. He'd often seen the man at the little bakery where Buzz stopped for coffee on his way to the mountain. He'd struck up a conversation with the man after a respectable amount of time. Heath wasn't tight-lipped necessarily but didn't seem to trust anyone either.

He'd been a warden for more than a year when he'd first busted Heath for poaching. The man had insisted he had ancestral blood, was part of the Abenaki tribe. But when asked for documentation, couldn't produce it. From there Buzz and Vernon Heath's relationship had gone from prickly to downright hostile. Buzz had dug deeper into the man's past after Heath had threatened him a couple of years back. That was when Buzz had learned about the group Heath was part of. He'd shared the information with Craig, who'd looked into the man further.

"Yup, your instincts were right on," Craig had said, giving Buzz an air toast with a glass of dark lager. "Man's nuttier than Grandma's fruitcake."

Heath was part of a group that appeared to be some sort of cult. He and some others met quarterly, Craig had said. Always in the same location. Always the same people. Always on the third Sunday of the first month of the quarter.

Craig had gone so far as to talk to Heather, his sister, into gaining access. She'd struck up a friendship with one of the women—not hard as Heather was a talker with girl-next-door good looks—and had eventually found out more about the group.

Witchcraft and curses and of all things, giant man-eating bats were what it had boiled down to. Buzz hadn't gotten all the details—in fact, he wasn't sure Heather had—but enough to know that Heath and the others were hunting these big bats in and around Groton and other wilderness areas.

***

"Hello, sunshine," Craig greeted Buzz as he climbed out of the Jeep. "Nice of you to make it."

Buzz grinned and thumped Craig on the shoulder. "Thanks for coming."

"Wouldn't miss it. Chance to shoot something other than targets and skeet?" Craig rolled his shoulders. Though he sported a slight beer belly from all the pub crawls, he was still in good shape. Like Buzz, Craig probably still made his bed with tight corners and ironed his shirts as soon as they'd finished tumbling in the dryer.

"So, what's the plan?" Craig asked.

"Well, here's what I'm thinking." Buzz spread the map of the forest and surrounding campgrounds out on the hood of his vehicle. He jabbed at the spot he'd outlined in pencil from the map Jude had given him.

"We found the family here. The boy says that they came from this area," Buzz pointed to a tight knot of trees where the forest started to incline. "That," he pointed at a tiny red "x" he'd made, "marks the spot. It's a cavern. Supposedly where Heath was headed."

"Giant bats like caverns. Makes sense to me." Craig grinned. He lifted the grungy cap off his head, showing off a barely-there hairline, and slapped it back down. "You ready?"

Buzz grinned. "Born that way."

"Then let's go."

***

The tangled undergrowth and thick trees made traversing the forest a challenge. It had been strange coming from a desert into the thick wilderness of New England. At first, Buzz had found it disorienting, even—though he'd never admit it—frightening. It was like walking in a house of mirrors. Everything started to look the same. But the more time he'd spent outdoors in all seasons, the more he'd come to not only appreciate the beauty of the landscape but also to understand it.

The outdoor survival classes he'd taken had been invaluable. As had the extra workshops and expeditions he and either Jennifer or Craig had gone on with him. Buzz felt like he'd had a crash course in the wilderness of Vermont over the past few years. At times like this, he appreciated it.

He used the map and his compass religiously. It was much too easy to get misplaced out here, even for experienced hikers and backpackers. He never trusted his GPS unit. Too much tree cover or other interference made the signal dicey at best.

"Shouldn't be much further," Buzz said when they'd paused to suck down some water. "I'd estimate another half hour at most."

"Half hour in your time or mine?" Craig asked. "Listen, man, in all seriousness," Craig's smile slipped off his face. "What will we be dealing with?"

Buzz shook his head. "I'm not sure. At best? Breaking up an ineffective bat hunting party."

"Looney tunes, huh?" Craig paused and wiped the back of his hand over his mouth. "Remember the stuff Heather said they talked about at their meetings? Witches and curses and black magic and beasts from folklore come to life."

"Yeah."

Craig shook his head. "Sad. To have lost your grip on reality like that. I wonder what happens to people?"

"I don't know." Buzz had been wondering the same thing. Desperate people, he thought, people who have "issues" Jennifer would say, that they haven't dealt with.

"Let's get there in twenty," Craig said, capping his water bottle and thrusting it back into his pack. Buzz saw the black handgrip of the Ruger his friend wore constantly and nodded.

"Sounds good to me."

This time they ran through the woods, dodging low-hanging branches and twisted, fallen logs. It took them twenty-three minutes to reach the little clearing outside of the cavern. Both were panting, Craig a little heavier than Buzz, he noted with a little sliver of pride.

A quick look around confirmed that this was the place. Buzz found prints from the family, along with signs of a sleeping area and cold fire.

"So where is it?" Craig asked.

Buzz consulted the map again and jabbed a finger up at a tall-looking pile of rocks on the slope above them. "Looks like that's our twenty."

They made their way up. The rocks and stones were slippery, the ground uneven. Twisted, stunted shrubbery clung to the side of the steep hill as though holding on for dear life. When they reached the top, they both paused again after ducking inside the entrance. It was dark inside, musty and damp feeling. Sweat trickled down the sides of his face as Buzz double-checked his pistol in its holster and the knife on his leg sheath.

"Ready?" he asked his friend.

"Hell yeah," Craig said and led the way deeper into the tunnel.

Chapter 31

Vernon Heath

Vernon collapsed onto his side. It'd gotten him. He couldn't believe it. Even though he'd gone into the cavern knowing that it was a possibility he might not get out, he hadn't understood, hadn't fully grasped it as reality.

He turned, looked at his arm again. Three deep, oozing gouges crossed his upper arm. A wave of dizziness washed over him. He felt heat like he'd opened an oven door and climbed inside, knew he was sweating. His lips were still shaking when he clamped them together.

To distract himself, Vernon turned his head. There was Geoffrey. The younger man cowered beside a rock, hidden from the sight of the two giant bats that swooped overhead. The strange hissing sounds were still coming from their ugly gray-lipped mouths. Vernon could see the jagged teeth the size of a dog's, from where he lay when they swooped close.

Like Geoffrey, Vernon had wedged himself into a makeshift covering. Unless the bats landed directly on the big stone above and were able to shove their heads through the opening, Vernon would be all right. Geoffrey...well, Vernon didn't much care what happened to Geoffrey. The man was worthless. Vernon might as well have let a group of Girl Scouts tag along in his place. At least they'd bring cookies, he thought bitterly.

He looked around the cavern. How the hell was he going to get out of here? The way up the ravine, where they'd come in was out of the question. The bats would pick him off before he made it a quarter of the way up. Not to mention trying to do it one-handed. Where else then? He scanned the area but the big rock protecting his head also made it impossible to see behind him. He'd have to get his eyes clear of the stone overhang if he wanted to get a full lay of the land. He shuddered thinking about it. He didn't want any part of him exposed to those talons again.

Digging in his pack, Vernon extracted a dirty thermal shirt. He gritted his teeth, knowing what had to be done was going to be agony. Would he piss himself? he wondered. He hoped he wouldn't pass out. Awkwardly, he folded the shirt with his good hand into a long tube, then draped that over his upper arm. Fire raced up and down the wounds and Vernon had to stop a second to get his breath back. It had to be done. He needed to stop the bleeding or he'd have worse problems to deal with. A wave of nausea crested in his belly as he pulled the shirt tighter and then tighter again. He closed his eyes and waited for the sick feeling to pass or to puke.

The bats were still hissing but...was it getting quieter? Further away? He waited for another three breaths, then slowly, cautiously raised his head.

"They're leaving," Geoffrey said in a stage whisper. "Going out that way." He jabbed his arm toward the side of the cavern furthest from where they were hiding. Geoffrey's entire upper body was exposed to the open air. Vernon made a slashing motion at his throat. *Shut up,* Vernon thought, *before you get us both killed.*

The smaller bats that had lined the ceiling earlier were swooping down to Tess, or what was left of her. Vernon didn't look. Was glad that another large stone hid her body from view. Some of them flew around the cavern erratically, and every so often when one flew in his general direction, Vernon felt a strange, electrical-like current.

Stupid or not, Geoffrey was right about the big bats. They made circles closer and closer to the other side of the cavern. Vernon watched in relief as first one and then the other made tighter loops and then finally ducked and flew down a passageway that he couldn't see.

He moved into a crouch, scanned the rest of the room before dropping back into his hiding spot. Across from him, maybe twenty-five or thirty feet was an opening. Did it go out? He had no idea. But it left this room or seemed to. And anything had to be better than being trapped here. *Unless it's a dead-end,* a little voice whispered in his head. *Then what?*

Vernon raised himself and looked around again, slower this time. There weren't any other exits, at least none he could see. He was going for it. He motioned to Geoffrey, pointed toward the hole. A loud hiss sounded near Vernon's head and he swung around. One of the smaller bats was perched on the rock directly beside him. Its ugly mouse-like face smushed in like a pug's. It opened its mouth, its breath rank. Vernon slipped the knife out of his leg sheath and jerked his arm upward. The thing screamed as the knife cut it in half. Blood sprayed Vernon's face and he rubbed his good arm over his face hastily, cleared his eyes.

The bat's death cry had caught the attention of many of the

other bats in the cavern. Their heads perked up, triangular ears raised. The glittering eyes of hundreds of the tiny winged beasts turned toward him.

Vernon held his wounded arm close to him and charged toward the opening in the wall. His right knee hit a rock and he grunted. Pain raced up his thigh. He scrabbled over stones, the knife still in his good hand. He was getting closer, twenty feet now, maybe fifteen. Behind him, the bats' wings beat at the air like a thousand tiny propellers. Geoffrey yelled something. Vernon couldn't hear it over his rasping breath. His lungs burned, his injured arm screamed at him as he jostled it, climbing over stones and nearly falling down rock faces.

Ten feet.

Two bats pinwheeled by his head and he ducked his head rather than lashing out with the knife again. He would fall if he tried and he couldn't. Not now. He kept his eyes focused on the opening. Geoffrey yelled something else. Was he being attacked? Trying to tell Vernon to wait for him?

Five feet.

Vernon saw the opening more clearly now. It was smaller than he'd thought. Big enough to cram himself into? He thought so. Plunging forward, the hand with the knife straight out in front of him, he half-clutched rocks and stones. He heaved himself up and over the biggest ones in front of the opening. Flattened himself back down. Tried to stay low, stay out of the bats' airspace.

Two feet.

A tiny bat—the smallest he'd seen—flew out of his right field of vision. Vernon saw it swoop toward him then screeched and flew away before diving back down.

Vernon dove into the tunnel. It was darker here, tight. It

smelled of damp earth. He turned as quickly as the narrow space would allow, put the knife hand out. Ready to strike. A big, dark shape loomed in the opening.

"Let me in," Geoffrey yelled.

Vernon hesitated, then pulled the other man into the tight space beside him.

"Look out!" Geoffrey yelled. A medium-sized bat made a dive-bomb for Geoffrey's head. Vernon swatted with his hand, knocked the bat off-kilter. It quickly righted itself though and bared its teeth, snarling. Vernon reached over Geoffrey's cowering form and jabbed at the bat with the knife. It fell with a screeching moan to the rocks underfoot.

"We've got to get out of here!" Vernon yelled.

Geoffrey stared at him dumbly.

"Come on." Vernon turned and pushed into the darkness of the tunnel.

Chapter 32

Buzz Matthews

It felt strange to be inside the ground. Here, every sound was muted like the air itself was thick, sludgy. The humidity from outdoors had abated though, the cave walls putting off a refreshingly cool mist. Had this cave, like so many others in the state, been used by bootleggers? It was far out though, to be of any real use. Stones clinked together underfoot though he and Craig walked slowly.

Buzz checked his watch. It had been twenty minutes. So far, no sign of Heath.

"How much further in do you think it goes?" Craig asked softly. His headlamp wobbled. As he turned toward Buzz, Craig lowered his head slightly, to keep the bright light from blinding him.

"Not sure. Can't be much further, can it?"

Craig grunted. "Who knows?"

They walked in silence for what felt like a long time. Then Craig stopped abruptly, held up his arm. Buzz froze.

"There's the "v" that the kid told you about," Craig motioned, his arm stretched up above them. Buzz's eyes followed Craig's headlamp.

"There's the opening," Buzz said quietly and pointed toward a spot high up on the tunnel's wall. A small piece of red fabric moved there, some underground breeze making it shimmy and shake.

They climbed up single file, Buzz in the lead now. He took his pack off, poked his head and shoulders through the opening. His headlamp shone down into an abyss. He whistled quietly under his breath. It looked like a cliff face, only slightly tilted so that one could climb down if very careful and taking one's time. Rocks littered the walls. At least there would be places to put his feet, things to hold onto. He shone his headlamp around him but didn't see any signs of bats large or small. They'd been here though, the smell of guano was so thick it made his eyes water.

"How's it look?" Craig asked from behind him.

"Steep," Buzz said. He pulled his head back into the tunnel and waved at Craig to have a look.

Craig too whistled. "Stinks. Any other way in?"

Buzz paused, then shook his head. "I don't think so."

"Looks like we should have brushed up on our rock-climbing skills," Craig said with a slow smile. "You first?"

Buzz nodded. They eased their bodies through the tight opening—Craig almost getting stuck at one point and needing a hand—then pulled their packs through. They picked their way carefully over the rocks and stones, trying hard to remain quiet. The air beneath the guano was flat and lifeless though and Buzz heard wind moving through the space. He wondered where it came from. He was about to turn and ask Craig if he heard it too when something caught his eye. A movement to the left. He turned and the light beam from his headlamp illuminated the erratic flapping wings of a bat nearby. Craig

219

ducked and Buzz did the same. But rather than flying up higher, as bats usually did, this one dive-bombed. Craig fumbled with his knife, tried to unsheathe it. Buzz, reached up and knocked the bat away from Craig's head with a quick, downward motion. The little furry body sailed through the air and back into the darkness.

"Thanks, man," Craig said.

Buzz grunted in response and they kept walking

"Think that was the giant bat Heath's looking for?" Craig asked a minute later, laughter laced his voice.

Buzz snorted. "Maybe."

The rock wall to their right had gotten steeper. They moved in a crouch, keeping their bodies low to the ground in case they lost their footing. Occasionally, one or both of them put a hand out to get their balance on the steeply pitched rocks underfoot. The stone under Buzz's hand was damp and cool, but this whole cavern was not as cold as the tunnel that had led them here. Strange. You'd think being further underground it would be even colder. That it might—

"Look out!" Craig said.

Buzz stopped.

"Left, to your left!"

Buzz swiveled to his left, his knife already in hand. A bunch of bats—not enough to be a colony but more than a handful—swooped toward him. Buzz lashed out with his arm when they drew closer. Craig did the same. The bats' wings beat the air around their heads, too close for comfort. Their furry bodies were illuminated by his light. They were gray rather than brown. Their faces were ugly like pressed in monkeys. The one closest to Craig hissed and showed its sharp teeth. Craig swatted it out of the way with his hand and then yelped.

"It bit me," he said in a surprised voice. "The little shit bit me." He stared for a second at his hand. Two little trickles of blood flowed out of the meaty part near his thumb.

"Behind you, man." Buzz swatted away the last of the small bats. A tennis racquet would have been a better choice than the knife. The little bat tumbled over and over in the air before swooping off toward some lower part of the cavern.

Craig turned and punched at the bat that had flown down near the back of his head. It too fell from the air and unlike the other didn't correct its downward path fast enough. Buzz heard the small thud it made as it connected with the rock floor beneath them.

"What is up with this?" Craig asked. He shook his bitten hand and then his head. "Stupid things."

There was more movement ahead of them. Buzz nodded toward it. "Looks like more coming."

Craig followed his gaze and swore. He swung his head around to say something to Buzz. When he did the beam of light touched on something beneath them and to the left. What had it been? Buzz was about to turn his head in that direction but the small group of mean little bats was already descending. Using their knives and fists, Buzz and Craig cleared the air again.

Afterward, Craig breathed heavily. Buzz's own heart thumped hard in his chest.

"I saw something," Buzz said, and swung his light toward the cavern's floor. It wasn't far now—maybe three yards from where they were standing. At first, his light picked up only rocks and stones and more rocks.

But then—there it was again. A flash of red.

"There's something down there," he said.

Craig nodded, wiped a hand over his face. "Let's go down and see." He motioned for Buzz to lead the way. Buzz scanned the air around them, waiting for the next group of rabid bats to descend.

Why would they behave so weirdly? And why did they look like...mutants? Vermont's bats were brown, furry, and fairly cute if you didn't mind rodents. Besides, bats were usually afraid of humans, staying clear of them. Sure, they'd bite people or other animals if they were threatened. But that happened when they were hemmed in. They'd lash out in panic, bite someone or something trying to get free. But why here? He and Craig weren't acting aggressively toward them.

"How's the hand?" Buzz asked. But Craig's answer was lost as he clambered over the next large stone. Buzz blinked away the powerful ammonia sting of the guano that filled his nose and burned his eyes. And then he saw what the flash of red was. A body. Or what was left of one.

Craig cursed from behind him. "What the hell happened here?" Craig asked.

Buzz wanted to look away. The sight before him made the short hairs at the back of his neck stand on end. What had happened here? Someone—an unlucky woman or man—had fallen to his or her death. But what had happened to the body afterward? Had the bats done this? Buzz shook his head in slow motion. No way. No way that was possible. What was left of the figure looked like it had been eaten by a bear. Or three.

"To your left!" Craig yelled.

Buzz didn't have time to respond before Craig slammed into his back, throwing him to the ground. Buzz fell to the rocky ground, his ribs banged painfully against a sharp stone. Craig lay half on top of him. He rolled off and drew his gun.

"Look!" Craig's voice was loud, tense. "There, it's coming back!"

Buzz rolled onto his back and drew his gun too. The scent of blood and other interior body smells filled the air and he gagged. What did Craig see? Buzz peered up but saw only the ceiling far away.

And then…something. He blinked, squinted. *That's not possible,* a little voice inside chimed.He squinted harder but it was still there. A bat the size of a medium-sized dog. Its wings swatted the air overhead. It had the same ugly, smashed-in face as the smaller bats, this one at least six inches across. It bared its teeth and swooped toward Craig and Buzz.

Buzz twisted, tried to get his feet under him. His hand shook slightly as he aimed the gun toward its head. The bat made a loud hissing sound. The air around Buzz pulsed. It was strange, like all the light and sound and feel of the room was gone for a second before it returned. He was paralyzed like he'd been electrocuted at the same time he'd lost all feeling in his body.

A shot blasted. The tip of Craig's gun smoked. The sound roared through the space. And then the giant bat screeched and fell to the left, a huge, gaping hole in its wing.

"Move, move!" Craig yelled. And suddenly Buzz was back in boot camp, his instructor yelling at him to *go, go, go!* His training took over. He hunched low and ran over the stones and rocks. He scanned the rocks where the bat had fallen every couple of seconds until Craig shoved his back.

"Just go!" Craig yelled.

Across the wide cavern was a dull glowing light. Buzz ran

toward it. Didn't know what it was but needed to get out from the open. Get to cover. There was something there. Maybe a niche in the rock or another tunnel? The rocky surface of the cavern's floor made it hard to move quickly. He went as fast and as hard as he could. Craig huffed behind him.

Through the gloom, Buzz saw a huge, strange stone that almost looked like a table. He registered things on it—white cylinders, maybe candles?—but didn't stop. Behind him came another sound, wings flapped through the stale air. Buzz looked back.

"Look out!" he yelled.

The bat had risen and was within feet of Craig who turned, startled. The bat swooped and another strange blast of current filled the air. Buzz raised his hand, struggled to move. The air was charged and thick, like pea soup laced with lightning. He fired the gun, not at the bat directly. It was too close to Craig. It hissed in response and then screeched. Immediately, it jerked up and away from Craig.

"Go, go!" Craig said, his face white in the wash of Buzz's headlamp.

"You okay?"

"Go!"

Buzz swept his arm forward, motioning for Craig to go ahead of him. "I'll take the rear," he said. Craig hesitated, then nodded and plunged in front of Buzz.

They were near to the other side of the cavern now. Buzz paused, still ducked low, and scanned the air behind them. Nothing. The bat, he realized now, the one that had just dive-bombed them, hadn't had a bad wing. There had to be two of them. Two. Maybe more? Buzz looked around again, still stumble-running after Craig.

He hit his knee against a stone, skinned his palms on another as he climbed over it. His breath came hard and fast in his chest. They were close though.

Almost there.

The light Buzz had seen earlier had faded, but Craig's headlight illuminated a hole in the wall, a tunnel of some sort.

A way out? *Please, God, let it be a way out.* All the thoughts of Jennifer he'd been pushing into the background surged forward in his brain. Then, wham! Another of the strange paralyzing jolts hit him. The rocks around him shook with the force of it, clinking and skittering together. He stumbled, caught himself on a big boulder. Then ducked behind it and surveyed the rocks.

The bat was back. Its wingspan was incredible—Buzz couldn't help but marvel—before he shook himself into action. He raised his handgun, arms slow and heavy. This time he took careful aim. The bat's ugly gray face snarled as it drew closer. He wanted to be closer to it though. He couldn't afford to miss it.

"Shoot!" Craig yelled. Buzz adjusted his aim and fired. One shot, two. The noise reverberated around the rocks and stones. Immediately Buzz's ears rang so loud he couldn't hear anything else.

He'd hit it though. Hadn't he?

"You got it," Craig said, breathing hard. He'd backtracked a couple of feet to Buzz's side. It sounded like Craig was underwater.

Buzz shook his head. "Not sure," he panted. "I think so."

"Good shot. I'm ninety percent sure you took it out. Come on, let's keep going."

Buzz noticed a movement from the left side of his vision. He jerked and saw a bat, the one with the damaged wing, careen brokenly from one rock to another.

It drew closer.

Its body was the same color as the stone and it moved erratically, barely staying in place long enough to set its talons down before it scrabbled to another stone and hiding from view.

"You go," Buzz said to Craig. "I'm going to get this one."

"No way, man. I'm here till the bitter end."

Buzz smiled, edging toward the place the second bat had gone down. He swept the area with his headlamp.

Nothing.

Then a loud hiss to his right.

Craig reacted first, drawing his gun. The injured bat was only a few yards away. It seemed to duck away from the light though when Craig advanced. Were they bothered by the light? Buzz wished suddenly he had a truckload of spotlights. He'd light the place up. That'd make this whole thing a lot easier.

"He…hello?" a voice called. Buzz turned while Craig kept his gun trained on the last spot the bat had stood.

The voice had come from somewhere in front of them. Was that the light Buzz had seen?

"This is Buzz Matthews. I'm the game warden in this area," he said in a loud, clear voice.

The light in the tunnel grew brighter. A head poked out of it seconds later. A man, light hair, in his early fifties raised a hand against the light.

"I'm Geoffrey—"

"Get back in there until I say it's safe to come out," Buzz said, his voice calm but authoritative. Jennifer called it his mad dad voice. "Please, sir."

The man nodded, hesitated a second before retreating.

"Got a line on it?" Buzz asked Craig softly when he'd picked his way back over the rocks to his friend's side.

Craig shook his head. "Thing won't come out. I may have to go up and over," he nodded toward where they'd last seen the bat lurking. "See if I can't—"

Suddenly the bat appeared, flying jerkily up from a small crevasse close to where the men stood. It screeched, the sound deafening. Then it dove toward Craig. He put his arm up instinctively, protecting his face and head with his forearm.

The bat's talons reached out, like a big waterbird swooping down to collect a fish. Buzz fired his gun. *Too close,* he thought, *too close to Craig.*

But there wasn't any other choice.

The talons missed Craig by centimeters. The bat, blown backward by the force of the bullet, lay in a crumpled heap in the rocks. Craig stood stock still another full minute before he lowered his arm. He looked from the bat collapsed on the ground in front of him, to Buzz, then back to the bat.

They stood in silence a minute longer, the only sound in the quiet space their labored breathing.

"You all right?" Buzz asked. Craig only nodded.

"Is…is everything okay?" a timid voice called out from the tunnel. Buzz and Craig exchanged a glance.

The two men walked slowly to the tunnel's entrance.

"I'm Geoffrey," the pale man said. "Geoffrey Masters. Did you…did you kill them?"

"Yes, sir," Buzz said when the two had drawn close enough to the tunnel to speak in regular voices. "I believe we did. Are you all right? Any injuries?"

Geoffrey shook his head. "No, I—we're fine."

"We?"

"An… acquaintance and I. We're fine."

"You both need to come out of there," Craig said and nodded toward the tunnel. Geoffrey hesitated. Then he nodded and retreated into the tunnel.

Craig looked at Buzz and laughed. It was shaky. "Hell of a thing, huh?" he asked. "Wouldn't believe it if I didn't see it with my own eyes."

Buzz nodded, holstering his gun and using his shirt to wipe the sweat off his forehead.

The men surveyed the area, then took turns getting drinks from their packs. Buzz's throat was as dry as dirt.

"We bringing them back for study?" Craig asked.

Buzz nodded. "Absolutely."

Craig grinned. "We'll be the talk of the scientific community."

Rocks clinked together in the tunnel and then Geoffrey re-emerged.

"I—well. It appears that my, ah, acquaintance has left."

"Just where the hell did she go?" Craig asked, his voice dropping an octave.

Geoffrey cleared his throat. "It's not her, it's a him. And I don't know. He appears to have just…vanished."

Buzz's eyes narrowed. "Your friend wouldn't be Vernon Heath, would he?"

Geoffrey swallowed, glanced away from Buzz, and then back. "I wouldn't call him a friend."

Buzz shook his head then glanced at Craig.

"Where's that tunnel go?" Craig asked Geoffrey.

"I'm really not sure. Gentlemen, I very much need to get

out of this…this place. My friend, Tess was killed…" his voice turned trembly and he paused a second, pressed his lips together before continuing. "She was killed here. Her family…We need to notify the authorities. Well, it seems you are the authority," he motioned with his hand toward Buzz. "And I'm sorry, I don't believe I caught your name," he looked at Craig.

Craig just stared back at him. Geoffrey finally fell silent.

"What's the plan?" Craig asked Buzz quietly.

Buzz put a hand to the back of his neck and rubbed. He was close to Heath. He should go in and check the tunnel himself, make sure that Geoffrey wasn't lying. On the other hand… there was a civilian here that needed to be kept safe. And, he had to admit, he was anxious to bag the bats and bring them to the lab. And the woman—Tess?—needed to be removed from the area, her next of kin notified. A wave of guilt swept over Buzz. That should have been his first thought. In all the excitement he hadn't been thinking clearly. The woman's family deserved to know what happened and Geoffrey was right, the coroner and State Police would need to be notified about the body.

Buzz clapped a hand on Geoffrey's shoulder. The pale man jumped, startled.

"Let's get you home," Buzz said. Craig nodded and took the lead, Geoffrey sandwiched between the two men in a single-file line.

Chapter 33

Buzz Matthews

They hadn't had bags or anything else to carry the dead bats out of the cave with. So, while waiting for backup, Craig had stayed with Geoffrey and Buzz had gone back into the cave. He'd left chalk marks on the stones on their hike out, to make finding the way easier. He half-expected to run into Heath but saw no one. Craig was going to send the coroner in when she arrived, and the EMTs were on their way as well. They'd check out Geoffrey who'd nervously insisted he was fine, and could he please just leave now?

"After you've been checked out," Craig had said, his voice not inviting question. "And questioned. The police will want to speak with you about…your friend. And what happened to her."

Geoffrey had stood nervously by the stone Craig sat on, fiddling with the zippers on his vest, sighing, and wiping his eyes intermittently. In addition to being sad, Buzz realized that Geoffrey was embarrassed. He wanted to get out of the area with the least amount of people possible knowing he'd ever been there.

Now, Buzz spotted the flare he'd left at the top of the cavern's steep drop off. The reddish light made strange shadows on the cave's walls. Buzz descended quickly, his pack lighter now that it was filled with only a first aid kit and his retrieval tools: thick plastic bags to put the bats' bodies in, along with a good camera for photographing them in the dim environment. He'd also brought along the kit he used to measure tracks and the logbook. He could just picture his supervisor's face when he brought in the bats.

He left a wide berth around the body on the ground and glanced overhead out of instinct. There was movement at the top of the cavern's ceiling. His heart pounded as his headlamp picked out the carpet of furry bodies up above. A lot of these bats—the normal brown variety—were hated by people but Buzz had never been bothered by them.

Following the chalk marks, Buzz retraced his steps. He'd made a large star on the stones near the bats' bodies to locate them easily. The first one was on a rock a few feet to the left. He veered in that direction, set his pack down. And frowned. The ground was clear. There were rocks, stones, pebbles.

But no bat.

Buzz double-checked the rock. The star was there. He looked around the other sides of the marked stone.

Nothing.

No animal dead or alive.

Not even a little tuft of fur.

But wait—what was that? He bent over. A thin trail of blackish liquid. Bat blood? He stuck his finger in it and drew it to his nose. It smelled metallic like blood but there was another scent mixed in. Something rancid.

Hurrying, Buzz moved to the next stone marked with a star.

It took him a second to find it. When he did, he again searched the area quickly. There was nothing there. He looked more carefully, spreading out from his initial location in widening circles.

Nothing.

Buzz felt a mixture of anger and disbelief rise. How...?

Heath.

If he'd been hiding in that tunnel, not run like Geoffrey had said, then he could have easily come out and bagged the bats himself. Taken them...where? Buzz cursed and stood up He searched around both the marked stones again, just in case. But no bat bodies, gigantic or otherwise, were anywhere. With a loud grunt of frustration, he hit the closest rock.

He should have checked the tunnel. Should have found Heath, taken him into custody. The man was a known poacher. He should be questioned by the police about the woman's death, too. If Buzz had trusted his gut he'd have both Heath and the bats now.

Anger and disappointment boiled in his belly. Buzz rolled his shoulders, tried to think. He could still go after Heath. Follow the tunnel where they'd found Geoffrey as far back as he could...

But what about the backup? As warden, it was his job to fill out the paperwork, assist the coroner with the collection of the deceased woman's remains, or at least make sure they didn't need additional help. The next of kin contact would be made by the police, but Buzz would be needed to share information with the State boys and fill out even more forms.

He swore again, but this time wisely punched his fist into his palm rather than a rock.

Jennifer would never forgive him if he went into that tunnel and never came out. Who knew where it even led? Was getting the bodies of the bats and bringing in a poacher worth his life? Maybe Heath had never been in there. All Buzz had was Geoffrey's word.

But something, or someone, had taken the bats' bodies. And if Buzz didn't find Heath, he might never get the answers to the questions he had. Buzz looked at the tunnel and then back at the red-lit cavern.

So what did he do: stay or go?

Chapter 34

Vernon Heath

I t had all been a lie.

Lies. Lies. Lies.

The word repeated itself in his brain as he walked, struggling to carry the heavy pack. He should feel a sense of relief. That the curse was false. That there was no such thing as generations of people—his own family and ancestors—suffering from the vengeance of a dead witch.

He cursed himself, feeling a hopeless, pressing discouragement.

If it was all lies then Mary died for nothing. If the legend wasn't true then all the deaths in the group were just random accidents. Debbie's child did just die because of a careless mistake or a misstep or because it was his time or because… who knew why? A cold shiver climbed Vernon's backbone.

He should feel free. The bats were dead. He had them here, proof that he and the others weren't crazy. He had them! But instead of feeling victorious, Vernon only felt a dull, depressing lead weight fill his gut.

Lies.

All of it. For the past twenty-plus years, Vernon had

dedicated his life to one thing and one thing only: finding the bats and breaking the curse. He'd trusted in it. Like a stupid kid, he'd believed that if he did everything needed to break the curse, things would be better. Be different.

Instead, he'd discovered he was just a fool. A dumb, gullible old man. He'd wasted hours, days, months on this quest. Mary used to tease him that the only thing he liked as much as sex and beer was the thrill of the hunt.

Well, now he'd found what he was looking for, hadn't he? And what had he gained? Nothing.

Anger, hot and red, clawed up Vernon's esophagus.

To hell with this. All of it. He was going to freeze the damn flying rodents, sell their carcasses to the highest bidder. And the journal. He'd sell that too, why not? But first, he'd break up the group. He pictured their faces when he called a special meeting. Imagined the looks of disbelief, shock even. Some of them wouldn't believe him, that the curse hadn't been real. Some wouldn't want to give up on their belief they were right, that what they'd believed in and trusted had crumbled to nothing more than a worthless pile of dirt.

Others would be relieved. They'd love the idea it'd all been a farce like they'd believed deep down. Those who'd been called the weakest members of the group were the realists. Vernon scoffed. Wouldn't they get a kick out of that? It was Vernon and Geoffrey and others who'd been in the group the longest, been the strongest believers and supporters—

The sound of something in the branches nearby interrupted Vernon's thoughts. He glanced over his shoulder. A few limbs swung but he couldn't see anything that had caused it. A deer maybe? No, the branches were too high up. He scanned the area again but didn't see anything.

235

Vernon continued walking. Dusk had fallen. The air around him was still and quiet, other than the occasional mosquito buzzing. Vernon didn't bother to wave them away. He felt tired now like the anger had been a physical thing that had attacked his body. His limbs were sore. Maybe he should sit down and rest. He was miles from the cavern now, miles from Matthews and his crony and the whining, pathetic Geoffrey. He'd stop. Maybe set up camp for the night.

A motion above where the trees had been shaking minutes before caught his attention. A handful of bats flew up and then over his head. They dove periodically, snapping up mosquitoes and other bugs. Vernon watched them impassively.

Bats. If he never saw another of the flying mice in his life it would be too soon.

One dove down close. Near enough Vernon could see its little gray body. The bat narrowly missed his head and then flapped its wings soundlessly upward. Vernon looked around the ground for a rock...then froze. Brown bats lived in Vermont, and northern long-eared ones. These were both native. They ate bugs and remained shy around humans. The bat Vernon had just seen though was gray.

Again, one of the small bats overhead swooped down. This time another followed. Vernon ducked as the gray bats flew low—too low—and then he dropped to the ground on his belly. He struggled to unclip the clasp of his bag. He had a slingshot in here, some smooth stones. He was a dead aim, had been practicing for months in the woods as he walked, and on the targets, he'd set up outside the cabin. He needed—

Burning pain ran across the back of Vernon's neck. He yelled, put a hand there. A wriggling body under his palm. He gripped it, threw it away from him. It soared through the air but caught the air under its wings and straightened its flight pattern. Blood ran down Vernon's neck.

He cursed, turned back to his bag, dumped it upside down. The crumpled wings of the huge bats were tangled around each other. He left them in a heap and searched through the rest of his belongings: the journal with blood smears on its cover, a flashlight, some food, a half-empty water canteen. The knife was gone but his hand closed over the soft leather of the slingshot. Below it was the little suede bag filled with stones. He struggled to get the lace around it undone. He'd tied it tight, not wanting it to come loose in his bag. His bloody fingers were slippery on the strings.

A hiss filled the air. Vernon glanced up, his hand still on the bag. Four of the six bats were perched on a nearby tree branch at eye level. They sat like birds, wings drawn close to their small bodies. Their eyes glittered as they watched him. Without moving his gaze, Vernon squeezed a small stone out of the pouch and loaded it into the slingshot. Then, with one quick move, he aimed and let it loose. It struck the little bat on the end. Vernon watched with glee as it fell backward off the branch, its noisy hiss turned into a small hiccup of pain. And then nothing.

The other two bats looked from their fallen comrade to Vernon. Then they both hissed and screeched loudly. The three others that had been circling descended, tiny talons extending toward Vernon.

With a yell, Vernon jumped up. He ran the slingshot and bag of stones still in his hands. He could hear them behind him, their wings nearly soundless as they batted the air, but their horrible hissing coming closer and closer.

Vernon's heart pounded in his chest. His neck burned

237

like lava had erupted there. He swerved left and then right, avoiding the trees. The woods were dense outside this small open meadow and Vernon ran toward them. Anything to put a barricade between himself and the bats.

He glanced over his shoulder.

Too close.

They were flying low and fast. Two had broken off from the group and were swooping, one to the right and one to the left. They were hunting, he realized in disbelief. Flushing out their prey.

Putting his head down, Vernon sprinted toward the forest. He was close now, thirty feet maybe? His legs ached but he'd make it. He'd get into the woods, as thick as he could. They wouldn't be able to find him. They wouldn't—

The sky up ahead was lightening. That was Vernon's last thought as he broke into the trees, running, running as fast as he could. He didn't pause when the ground beneath his feet turned into nothingness. He was like the stupid Roadrunner in the cartoons he'd watched as a kid. The earth was beneath his feet and then it wasn't.

As his body fell over the cliff he didn't have enough breath in his lungs to scream. He tumbled over and over through the air. His hands still clutched the worthless stones and weapon. *I can't believe it,* Vernon thought. *After all of it, this is how it's going to end...*

The ground rose before him. Too fast. His body was taut and hard, anticipating impact. He looked up away from it, not wanting to see it swallow him.

Above he saw five tiny dots swooping and circling as the colony of bats flew off into the distance.

Chapter 35

Jude Langlois

"Now Jude, do you remember the difference between fiction and non-fiction?" Mrs. Pelsky asked. She leaned over his desk from behind him, a habit he didn't like. He could smell old coffee and cigarettes on her breath and turned his head slightly for fresh air.

"Yeah. Non-fiction is true and fiction is made up."

"Right," Mrs. Pelsky said, smiling slightly. "And today's assignment is to write a non-fiction piece."

"I am," Jude said.

Mrs. Pelsky made a tsking noise in her throat (another habit Jude hated) and sighed. "Jude, we're not going to talk about this again. You know what the rule is in class, don't you?"

Which one, Jude wanted to ask. There were about eight thousand. How was he supposed to remember them all? He thought of his parents though, and their disappointed faces if they got another call from the school counselor.

"Yes," he said instead. "I know."

"What you write at home is your business. But here in class, when I give an assignment, I expect it to be completed. Now," Mrs. Pelksy said. "What about the research you did last week on the aardvark? Why don't you pull that out of your research folder and see if you can't get a little inspiration from it, okay?"

Jude nodded slowly. His teacher waited until he'd dutifully retrieved his folder from his desk and pulled out his notes on aardvarks before she wandered away to torment some other student.

Jude stared at the page but didn't see the words.

It had been months now, since they'd been back home, back to normal, as Mom kept saying. She said it in this funny, overly-bright way though, like she didn't quite believe it herself. Dad hadn't been back at work for two months after he got home from the hospital. He'd started slowly then, just a couple of hours a day. He was back full-time now but at least he wasn't there as much as before.

"Before" was like its own time period. In history, they'd been learning about B.C. and A.D., and to Jude, it felt like life was carved into the same two distinct time periods: before the trip and afterward.

Jude flipped to a clean sheet of notepaper and wrote "Aard-varks" in careful print with his pencil across the top of the page. Then he sat there, thinking.

Before the summer trip, Jude had been a pretty happy kid. Sure, his parents fought a lot. But when they weren't fighting they were pretty cool. And when they were Jude got away with all kinds of things he wouldn't have otherwise: long hours of video games, eating whatever he wanted whenever he wanted because Mom and Dad stayed away from each other; overnight trips to friends' houses. He'd especially liked staying at Peyton's. His parents were divorced and he said that it meant just when he was getting sick of one parent, it was time to go to the other's house. Jude wasn't sure Peyton liked it as much as he said though. Once, Jude had walked in on Peyton looking at a picture of his family when his parents were together and his eyes had been all red.

After the summer trip things had changed, Jude thought. Some for the good and some not-so-good. His parents got along really well. They went to see a counselor now once a week, and Jude stayed with his grandmother who fed him as many cookies as he could eat.

His mother was a lot less angry, which was nice. She also painted and drew much more than before. Sometimes she'd come out of her studio with paint splatters in her hair and a dazed look on her face. She'd even set up a little corner of the art room for Jude, complete with a small table, fresh pots of paint, nice markers, and pencils with extra-sharp tips.

Dad and Mom sat together on the back deck when the weather was good and they'd even bought a year-round hot tub that Dad and his friend had put in. Jude could only stay in for ten minutes, his mother said, because he was still a kid. But his parents would sit out in it for a long time with glasses of sour-smelling wine, talking, and looking at the stars. A lot of times they held hands and a couple he'd caught them kissing. It was kinda gross, but also made Jude feel good inside. Like a warm ball of sunshine glowed in his chest.

Things at school and in town had gotten weirder though, since the trip. The news about the giant bats had gotten out. Mr. Matthews and his friend had scoured the woods for the bodies of the bats they'd killed but hadn't ever been able to find them. They'd looked like fools in the paper, his grandmother had said, clicking her tongue in disapproval. Jude didn't understand why telling the truth made you look like a fool, but he hadn't said anything. His parents never

241

told his grandmother what they'd seen, at least not that Jude knew. His mother finally insisted they did not talk about it outside the house. "It's not that we're ashamed or that what happened wasn't real," she'd told Jude when he'd asked her why he couldn't talk about it anymore. "It's because people don't understand."

Mr. Matthews had let Jude start helping him out at the station once a week. On Sunday afternoons, Jude would help him on his rounds for three hours. Sometimes he got invited for a picnic with the warden and his wife Jennifer, who was hot. A few times they'd invited him to Sunday School at their church. It wasn't what Jude had expected—there were older kids like him and they did some cool stuff, not painting angels on cotton ball clouds or reading picture books like Peyton said.

Scout was doing good, too. He was so smart! Jude had taught him to bring back the ball after he'd thrown it, how to roll over and how to play dead. But Jude didn't want to teach Scout to beg. He thought that if he was a dog, he wouldn't want to have to do that. Plus, it made him think of Tim, or Vernon and how mean he'd been to Scout. Jude had promised Scout that he'd never be mean to him. He was his best friend.

That was really important too because Peyton and some of Jude's other friends hadn't wanted to hang out with him lately. At first, Jude had believed them, that they were just busy and couldn't come over, or that they had other things to do with their families. But when his mom and him had been doing groceries after school one day, Jude had seen Peyton's mom's face when she caught sight of them. She'd turned her head away and grabbed Peyton's hand, rushing off into the frozen foods so fast she'd left their cart behind. Jude had started to run after them but his mother had stopped him.

"Baby, some people...some people don't believe our version of what happened in the woods," she'd said. Jude had seen a hint of sadness in her eyes and the familiar two lines between her eyebrows. But then she'd smiled at him and hugged him. "But we're going to be just fine, right?" She'd squeezed him tight until he'd pushed her away hissing, "Ugh, Mom!" An older lady with a walker had smiled at her mother then, and Mom had smiled back.

Vernon Heath's backpack had been found a few weeks after Jude and his family had returned home. But the man himself hadn't been seen or heard from since. And that no one had ever found those dead bats that Mr. Matthews and his friend had killed. It was weird, Jude thought, that he'd leave his pack in the middle of the woods. There had been some black goop, Mr. Matthews had told Jude when he'd asked about the pack. That was all though, no other signs of bats, giant or not. Maybe the smaller bats had carried them off? Jude shivered when he thought of Tim—no, Mr. Heath—and the bats. Maybe he was still tracking them. Maybe he'd lost his pack because he'd had to follow them real fast. He'd rather think that than that Mr. Heath was dead, maybe being eaten by bats in that gross cave.

"Maybe he just wanted to get a fresh start," Mom had said brightly of Mr. Heath. But Jude had seen his father's face darken a little and his lips press together.

Dad still walked with a cane. He might for a long time, maybe forever, because of the damage done to his leg. He'd had to have a blood transfusion too, which meant they used some other person's blood and pumped it into your body. Jude didn't like to think about that, or the needles they'd stuck Dad with at the hospital. His father had been sick for a long time.

But now he was better.

Jude wrote carefully across the top of the page, "Aardvarks are cool animals because…" Then he stopped. He actually didn't think aardvarks were very cool. Especially not when compared to say, giant bats.

"Ten more minutes, class," Mrs. Pelsky said from the back of the room. Jude rolled his wrists around in circles and Carlos, who was sitting closest to him made a funny face at him.

"What are you doing your report on?" Carlos had just moved here and didn't have very many friends yet. Jude thought his glasses made him look funny and had heard some other kids on the playground calling him four eyes. It was mean but also a little funny even though Jude never joined in laughing at him.

"Aardvarks," Jude said.

Carlos nodded.

"How about you?"

"Bats," Carlos said.

At first, Jude thought the other boy was making fun of him. But Carlos didn't smirk or anything. And then Jude realized that Carlos had only been in school for a couple of weeks. Maybe the stories about Jude and his "bat family" hadn't spread to the other boy yet.

"My mother hates them," Carlos said. "My grandmother does too and all of my aunties. But I like them. They're cool, don't you think?"

Jude paused a long minute and then nodded slowly. "Yeah," he said.

Carlos smiled at him. "Want to be my partner for the reading reports?"

Jude nodded again. "Sure," he said. "And I have a story that you're gonna love. I'm going to write a book about it and print copies. I'm probably going to sell them to you know, like a publisher or movie company or something."

Carlos's eyebrows went up into his hair.

"Wow. Really? What's it about? The story?"

Jude smiled. "Bats." He leaned closer. "Giant, killer ones."

Carlos didn't laugh. And he didn't make that you're-so-stupid-to-believe-that face either. Instead, he nodded.

"Cool," he said. "I'm a pretty good artist. Maybe I can help you with the drawings for it."

Jude shrugged. "Maybe," he said and kept his voice chill. But he could already see it on the bookstore shelves, a thin black book with bright white letters, *Man-Eaters of Mount Crag*. In the corner, a giant bat, blood dripping from its fangs would hover in the background.

Author's Note

Though the bats depicted in this book are nightmarish, real bats are fascinating creatures. They are also important in our ecosystem. According to the National Park Service, bats pollinate plants, eat insects, and serve as prey for other animals, among other important roles.

Unfortunately, a deadly disease, White-Nose Syndrome, has negatively impacted the bat population in recent years. Millions of bats across the U.S., have died from this disease according to statistics from the White-Nose Syndrome Response Team. Learn more about it on their website, www.whitenosesyndrome.org.

Osmore Pond Recreation Area is a real place in the Northeast Kingdom of Vermont, but I took liberties with the names of hiking trails and mountains in the area. Remote camping at the recreation area can be found and as in the book, campsites must be hiked or canoed to.

Though all the novels in the "Monsters in the Green Mountains," series contain scary things happening to people deep in remote wilderness areas, I hope this doesn't discourage you from being in the woods. Hiking, biking, canoeing, walking, snowshoeing, skiing—these are just a few of the many fun and exhilarating activities to enjoy with family and friends year-round. Better health, peace of mind, and happy memories are a few of the many benefits you'll experience.

Outdoors is one of my favorite places to be and where I feel most connected to God and sure of my place in the world. My hope is that you will experience that for yourself and fall in love with nature. But maybe leave your copy of *The Pact* at home!

Where it All Began...

Start at the beginning of the "Monsters in the Green Mountains" series with, *Silence in the Woods*.

In 1917, four friends and photojournalists set out in the woods looking for answers. Why have so many hikers and hunters gone missing in the area of Shiny Creek Trail?

The two couples anticipate a great adventure, one they'll tell their kids about someday. No one imagines the evil lurking in a remote cave. A horrifying discovery leaves one person dead and two others missing.

Two months later, Paul, one of the four, returns to the forest to find his wife. But will he find her before someone—or something—finds him?

About the Author

J.P. Choquette is the author of thriller novels set in Vermont. Her books, "turn pages, not stomachs," and frequently tie in the themes of art, nature, folklore, and psychology. She is a member of International Thriller Writers.

A lover of Gothic books and movies, J.P. enjoys being in nature with her family, spending time in old cemeteries, reading in the garden, and visiting junk shops. Sign up for the author's newsletter and receive a free short story.

You can connect with me on:
- http://jpchoquette.me
- https://twitter.com/jpchoquett
- https://www.instagram.com/jpchoquette_author

Subscribe to my newsletter:

✉ http://jpchoquette.me/free-story-newsletter

Also by J.P. Choquette

Other books by J.P. Choquette

Monsters in the Green Mountains
    Silence in the Woods
    Shadow in the Woods
    Under the Mountain

Stand-Alone Thriller Novels
    Let the Dead Rest
    Dark Circle
    Epidemic
    Subversion
    Restitution

Made in USA - Kendallville, IN
1219979_9781950976119
12.30.2020 1057